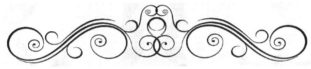

THE SHADOWS OF
STORMCLYFFE HALL

A DARK SEDUCTIONS NOVEL

THE SHADOWS OF
STORMCLYFFE HALL

A DARK SEDUCTIONS NOVEL

LAUREN SMITH

Entangled Publishing, LLC
2614 South Timberline Road
Suite 109
Fort Collins, CO 80525
Visit our website at www.entangledpublishing.com.

Select Otherworld is an imprint of Entangled Publishing, LLC.

Edited by Tracy Montoya
Cover design by Heather Howland
Cover art from iStock and Shutterstock

Manufactured in the United States of America

First Edition September 2014

For my mother, who gave me my first gothic romance novel and lit a supernatural fire in my blood, and for my father, who taught me to dance.

Prologue

The crash of thunder woke Richard, Earl of Weymouth. The fire in the hearth was low, the embers no longer crackling, and a cold draft pressed in around him as a storm raged outside. Pulling a loose sheet around his hips, he reached across the bed for his wife, who was still weak from bearing him a healthy son a month ago. His hands stopped short as he encountered nothing but the twisted sheets where her body had lain.

An icy tendril of fear churned in his stomach. She never left their bed when it rained. Storms frightened her. Isabelle usually curled into his side, burying her face against his throat for comfort.

Heavy rain whipped against the windows, the fierce staccato a warning to stay inside. Wind whistled through the room, teasing tapestries out, then back against the walls as though bodies moved behind them. A rumble of thunder seemed to shake the stones of his ancestral home, Stormclyffe Hall.

"Isabelle?" he called out. "Love?"

Only the crash of thunder answered.

Lightning streaked past the window and illuminated his son's cradle.

A sharp cry split the air.

Richard leaped out of bed, the icy floor stinging his bare feet as he rushed to the cradle. Murmuring soft, sweet words, he lifted his son, Edward, tucking him in the crook of one arm, relieved the babe was safe. He never thought he would be the paternal sort, but Isabelle and their babe brought out the tenderness in him.

The town viewed his marriage as a disgrace. Earls didn't marry the daughters of innkeepers. But Richard hadn't cared. He loved her and would do anything to have her in his life.

A frown tugged down the corners of his lips. "Where is your mother, Edward?"

Thunder once again rocked the hall. October storms thrashed the castle and nearby cliffs with a wicked vengeance. Trees were split in half by lightning; the edges of the cliff decayed inward, inching ever closer to the castle. Although the storm this night was no different, something felt wrong. A bite to the air, a sense of dread digging into his spine.

As the baby's long eyelashes drowsily settled back down on his plump cheeks, Richard assured himself that the baby's linens were dry and Edward was content. He brushed his lips over his son's forehead and set him back in the cradle.

When he stepped back, glancing out the window that overlooked the sea, his blood froze. A feminine silhouette clambered through the rock outcroppings by the cliff's edge.

Even from a distance, he knew with a horrifying certainty it was Isabelle.

It was madness to be outside, alone by the cliffs. She knew the dangers, knew the soft dirt around the cliffs crumbled into the sea. Only the year before, a boy from the village had fallen to his death when the ground by the edge gave way.

"Isabelle!" he gasped, the single intake of air burning his chest as though fire had erupted within.

Before he had time to move, the sky blackened, his vision robbed of light.

When lightning again bathed the rocks, Isabelle was gone.

His stomach clenched with a fear so profound, it flayed open his chest with poison-tipped claws.

Shouting for his cloak and boots, he raced from the room. The nurse emerged from down the hall, her white cap askew, and gray hair frizzing out from under the edges.

"Take charge of the baby!" he yelled as he ran past her.

She nodded and hurried to his room.

His valet, followed by several footmen, raced to his aid, carrying clothes. He snatched them and dressed as he ran, his men right behind him dashing through the deluge.

When they reached the cliffs, there was no sign of Isabelle.

"My lord!" a footman by the edge shouted.

Afraid to look, yet unable to tear his eyes away, Richard stared down to where the man's finger pointed. The black shadow of Isabelle's cloak caught on a razor-thin piece of rock, fluttering madly like a bat's wing. Lightning slashed above them, its terrible light revealing a dark smear beneath the cloak's erratic movements.

Blood. Isabelle's blood. Had she jumped to her death?

"*No!*" A crash of thunder swallowed his roar of despair.

He dove for the edge, wanting to follow her into the frothing gray seas. A cloak smeared with blood. All that remained of his wife.

He'd fought too hard to win her love, her trust. They'd suffered through too much together, to be divided now. He couldn't raise Edward alone.

"No...please, no." The pleading came from the bottom of his soul, torn from his heart.

She was gone.

Strong arms hauled Richard back from the ledge, pinning him to the earth.

"It is too late, my lord. She's gone."

She was his Isabelle, his heart…

Why had she jumped? Had she been unhappy? It couldn't be that. He would have known, and he would have done anything in his power to make her happy.

"We must find her," he told the men standing around him.

An older man, Richard's head gardener, shook his head. "We can't search in this weather, and her body will be gone by the time the storm ends. But we'll try to find what we can on the morrow, if you wish."

"I do," Richard growled. Despair was replaced with vengeance.

He faced Stormclyffe. Lightning laced the skies behind it in a white, delicate pattern. The centuries-old castle loomed out of the darkness, a defensive wolf with the battlements as its bared teeth.

It didn't matter that his infant son waited in a lonely cradle, eager for the loving touch of his remaining parent.

Richard was lost.

He wanted nothing to do with the life he'd had, the riches, the earldom. He despised it all. Every blessed memory he ever had that reminded him of Isabelle made him furious. She was gone from his life forever. He could not bring himself to dwell on his son; it only cleaved his chest in two. His love, his heart, was being battered against the rocks below.

Chapter One

Blood splashed against white porcelain, the ruby-red liquid spreading outward in a chaotic pattern.

Jane Seyton hissed, clutching her leg. The cut burned like the devil. She slapped a palm over the sliced flesh, but crimson liquid seeped through her fingers. She set down her razor and reached for the shower nozzle, aiming it at the red streaks, washing them down the drain. A thin trail of red still trickled down the tub's edge, and she blasted with the nozzle again, desperately trying to erase the unsettling sight of her own blood.

She hobbled out of the shower, rummaging through her makeup bag until she found a Band-Aid.

Her room in the tiny inn was quiet, the silence thick and a little unsettling. She hummed to break up the suffocating lack of noise.

It had been a tiring journey from Cambridge to the small, desolate coast near Weymouth in southern England.

The White Lady Inn had an almost macabre wooden sign, a silhouetted woman in white standing at the edge of a vast cliffside, her dress billowing out to sea in a cloud of smokelike swirls. It swung above the door and creaked with the slightest breeze. Despite the inn being situated between a lively pub and a quaint grocery store, there seemed to be a zone of quiet within the inn itself. Her room was a drab little place, with a narrow bed and whitewashed walls.

The same family had owned this inn for over two hundred years, passing it down from generation to generation. It was only natural that the place had seen better days and could use a little work. Yet, the awful silence made her skin tingle. She'd hardly slept last night, jumping at every small creak and groan. Taking herself to task, she'd consciously reminded herself that older places made such noises as the wood and stone settled into place.

Today she was driving up to the old castle-like manor house, Stormclyffe Hall, where she was going to meet the owner, the ninth Earl of Weymouth. After several emails back and forth, he'd reluctantly given her permission to tour the grounds along with other visitors but made no mention of getting access to the house's historical papers. Her dissertation was on the tragic stories of some of Britain's ancient castles and manor houses, with a particular emphasis on Stormclyffe and its effect on Weymouth. Her committee chair, Dr. Blackwell, had given her two weeks to find sources to supplement her theories on Stormclyffe Hall. Since the last four years of research footwork had been done on this one particular castle, she couldn't switch the focus easily to another location. If she couldn't get what she needed, she wouldn't get Blackwell's approval and she'd have to start her dissertation, for a PhD in history, over completely.

In order to complete her research, she had to find out what actually happened to the current earl's ancestors, Richard and his wife, Isabelle, who'd both died under mysterious circumstances. Rumor had it Isabelle had committed suicide. People claimed to have seen her ghost walking the cliffs. Richard had been found one foggy morning shortly thereafter sprawled in his study, a broken brandy glass next to his body. He had apparently drunk himself to an early grave a year after his wife's passing. The locals claimed the earl's spirit was trapped within the walls of his castle, restlessly searching for his dead wife, his mournful cries piercing the air on windless nights.

What Jane hadn't told the current earl or anyone else was the more personal reason for her focus on Stormclyffe Hall. Ever since she'd seen an old photo of it, she felt an almost mystical pull. Lately she couldn't seem to focus on anything else.

The hall whispered to her on the darkest of nights, with soft murmurs and teasing visions just as she began to fall asleep. Before dawn, she'd awaken, hands trembling with the feel of heavy stones against her palms, her heart racing and lips drawn back in a scream as though she'd fallen from the cliffs herself. What she felt, however, in each and every dream she had lately were hands shoving at her lower back, pushing her over the edge against her will.

The obsession with Stormclyffe had cost her so much already. The months of work on her dissertation were now at risk of being set aside if she couldn't find primary sources. It would be back to square one if she had to pick another castle and start all of her initial research over again, but that wasn't the worst of it. Her fiancé Tim had broken off their engagement and ended their two-year relationship, telling her he found her obsession with the castle "creepy" and that he worried she was mentally unstable.

But Jane's dreams made her wonder if the young countess hadn't jumped but been pushed by…someone. And that was the root of her obsession. The nightmares were slowly driving her mad, and she knew she had to get to the bottom of what happened to Isabelle if she ever hoped to find peace. She wasn't sure how much longer she could stand waking up every night gasping for breath and her bones aching as though they'd been smashed upon saltwater-covered rocks. The last few months she and Tim had been together, her dreams had grown increasingly vivid and terrifying, and they'd woken him up as well.

The beginning of the end.

She would never forget the look on his face, the tightness to his eyes and the way his lips pursed as he'd held out his hand and asked for his engagement ring back. His bags were packed and sitting by the door, and he'd left within minutes of destroying her life and all of her hopes for the future. *Their future.*

With a little sigh, she smoothed her left thumb over the base of her naked fourth finger. Even after four months, she still felt bare without it. A splinter of pain shot through her chest, and she clenched her fist, avoiding looking at her hand anymore. She rubbed a towel through her hair before blow-drying it. She could have used a flat iron to tame the mess of dark waves, but she'd fried that when she first arrived in England and plugged it into the wall socket with a converter that hadn't worked properly. She'd never gotten around to buying another one.

Not that it mattered. Given that her academic pursuits tended to involve panels of older, balding male professors in tweed jackets, she rarely bothered with her looks. Her current mission, though, required a more professional touch to her hair and wardrobe. She figured if she looked fashionable and presentable, it might help further her research goals. Easier said than done. She was fully aware she wasn't the sort of woman men fawned over, but her dissertation depended on access to the earl's family archives, and she'd get dolled up if it would help make sure he didn't change his mind about letting her pry into his papers.

The current earl had proved initially reluctant to allow her access to his family history, but when she'd persisted through a deluge of emails and letters, he'd reluctantly said she'd be welcome to tour the grounds along with other tourists once the remodeling was over. That had been four months ago. Stormclyffe didn't have a website to clue her in on whether the grounds were open to tourists or not, but the remodeling had to be done by now. She couldn't wait any longer. And she wasn't going to take no for an answer on getting into those original sources from the current earl.

A smile tugged at her lips.

Sebastian Carlisle, the ninth Earl of Weymouth. A rich playboy with the world at his fingertips. Of course he was tall, with gorgeous, dark blond hair like melted gold and eyes the shade of cinnamon. By all reports, his life consisted of fast cars, leggy models with perfect hair, and wealth beyond imagining. The man was definitely not her type, but she needed to impress him if she was to stay at the castle and work.

Her Internet searches also revealed a fair amount about him, aside from his romantic entanglements, and she'd been impressed. With a PhD in history from Cambridge and degrees in numerous foreign languages, he showed a surprising amount of scholarship. Despite his flashy lifestyle, he'd helped push for preservation of historical landmarks throughout Britain and was a member of the Royal Historical Society.

His town house in London was rumored to have one of the country's best library collections, second only to other collections in aristocratic homes like Althorp, home to the ninth Earl of Spencer. Even she had to admit that despite Carlyle's reputation as the most seductive man in all of

England, and he might also be one of the smartest.

She slipped into her favorite pair of jeans and a comfortable pair of black boots before donning a thick, gray, cable-knit sweater. Back home in Charleston, the weather would be light and warm, but the English coast was always cold in late October. Sea spray drifted far into town, sinking into her bones through the walls of the White Lady Inn.

Though it was still early afternoon, the sky outside her room dimmed as the low-hanging clouds drifted off the sea, dragging their vast looming shapes through the town and blocking out the sun's illumination. A chill seeped through the glass of the window, frosting the edges with dew that pebbled around the panes.

A sudden knot gathered at the base of her skull, the tiny hairs on the back of her neck rising. The air inside was now as cold as outside. Her breath exhaled in a cottony puff, and her skin tingled with a strange sensation. Her muscles tensed in response as though her body expected something to happen. If she hadn't known without a doubt that she was alone, she would have sworn someone was watching her.

She pushed the unsettling thought aside and retrieved her briefcase and purse. Tucked safely inside were her notebook and the latest letter she'd received last week from Sebastian Carlisle. She'd memorized every word.

Dear Ms. Seyton,

Thank you for your interest and inquiry into the Carlisle ancestral home, Stormclyffe Hall. As its caretaker and heir, I am very pleased that my ancestry has found merit in the esteemed Cambridge halls from where you write.

Your dissertation subject is a very interesting one, and

I do see how it might benefit your study to have access to my family's documents, and I would welcome your educated account of my home. However, I am currently overseeing the restoration of Stormclyffe, which includes the preservation of those documents that you seek, and having a scholar under the roof while that roof is being mended might prove distracting for both you and the restoration staff. You are more than welcome to visit once the restorations have been thoroughly completed. However, any access to personal and private papers and documents that are the property of my family are not open for public viewing. Weymouth has an excellent library with plenty of sources you might consider as an alternative avenue for research.

Please feel free to contact me, or the office of my steward Mr. John Knowles, in the future should you have any other questions.

Sincerely,
Weymouth

Jane's heart skittered. *Weymouth.* He hadn't even bothered to sign his usual title "Earl of Weymouth." Just *Weymouth.* It rolled off the tongue so nicely.

It had taken a half-dozen letters to his office and more than thirty emails to finally get his attention. His reply letter had been very British, polite and yet firm. It was obvious he didn't want her to come, at least not in her capacity as a researcher, but only as a tourist. *Ha!* He had no idea what he was in for. She was *going* to get into those documents.

The drive to Stormclyffe was beyond breathtaking. Weymouth was a charming harbor town, dotted with multicolored buildings that faced the edge of the water inlets like merry greeters. The forest of sailboat masts rose and fell as the sea rippled beneath the boats, lifting and dropping them in an endless waltz that enchanted her as she drove past. It was a place she could see herself living in for the rest of her life. She loved the idea of the cozy little place nestled next to the vast acreage of the Weymouth estate. She looked forward to leaving Stormclyffe on little breaks to pop down to the city and eat at the local pubs or visit the little shops and historical sites.

She drove past Weymouth Beach. The jubilee clock at the edge of the parking lot separated the beach from the shops and businesses. Its blue-and-red painted tower held the clock aloft for the residents to see the time at a distance. It painted a beautiful image, the clock at the edge of the shore, facing both sea and village. It stood as a silent sentinel over the flock of tourists that frolicked on the sand and in the shallows.

The twenty-minute drive to the estate took her on a narrow road that paralleled the edge of the coast. Although it was October, the grass was still green on the hillsides, and storm clouds were only a vague outline on the horizon. The landscape gave way to a slowly rising hill and a mass of distant trees, gnarled and knotted together tight as thorns. Just beyond was a glimpse of the castle. It was a massive edifice that stood stark against the sky and trees, towering over the fields, and she couldn't help but stare.

The countless photographs she'd collected over the years hadn't prepared her for the raw beauty and power of the structure. The worn battlements were still fully intact, facing the sea like warriors, ever defiant in the face of nature's force on the coast. The steep cliffs merely half a mile from the castle loomed, dark and threatening.

No fence lined the cliff edges. No warning signs guided visitors away except one that read PRIVATE PROPERTY. HEAVY

Fines for Trespassing. She repressed an achy shiver as a cloud stole across the sun's path, dimming all light.

The gray stones of Stormclyffe stood stalwart and proud, challenging her to drive closer. The road turned to gravel and thinned even more, leaving only enough space for her car.

Sheer desolation seemed to pour off the structure as she pulled into the castle's front drive. If not for the five work vehicles that obviously belonged to various handymen, she would have thought the castle was devoid of all life.

Strands of hair stung her face as the wind whipped it about. There was an unsettling silence on the grounds, like something unnatural muffled the sound of the sea. No crashing waves, only the violence of the wind against the castle's stones.

The house seemed to be wrapped in an invisible layer of thick wool, where sight and smell were dulled. The wind's icy fingers crawled along her shoulder blades and dug into her hair, making her tense with apprehension. The castle walls were pitted with small chinks in the stones like fathomless obsidian eyes that stared at her, sized her up, and found her wanting.

The hairs rose on the back of her neck. The eerie sensation of eyes fixed on her back sent a cold wave of apprehension over her skin. She whipped around to look at the deserted landscape, suddenly fighting off a rush of panic at being alone out here.

Her heartbeat froze for a brief moment. A woman in a long white nightgown, hair loose down to her waist, stood hesitantly on the cliff's edge, half turned toward the sea. She stared at Jane. Her skin was grayish, and her eyes were shadowed with black circles as though she hadn't slept in years. Something wasn't right about the way she looked, or the fact that the nightgown looked far too old in style for any modern woman to be wearing. Not to mention a woman in a nightgown in broad daylight wasn't right either…

Sadness filled Jane's chest, choking her. It was as if she were infused with the same lonely desperation evident on the woman's face. Surprisingly, Jane felt no fear, merely the overwhelming grief that had come the moment she locked eyes with the woman. As though pulled by an unseen force, she took a step in the woman's direction. The skies above darkened to a black, thunderous storm on the verge of breaking. Before she could get any closer, black roots burst forth from the rocks below the woman's slippered feet, winding up her calves and digging into her skin like thorns.

Jane had no time to react — her breath caught in her throat as the woman's eyes widened. Jane struggled to move, but her body wouldn't obey. Every muscle was tensed and yet frozen like stone. The woman opened her mouth, a silent scream ricocheting off the insides of Jane's skull. Then the thorny roots pulled her off the edge of the cliffs and into the sea.

"No!" A gasp escaped Jane's lips, barely above a whisper. Her skin broke out in goose bumps, and she shook her head, trying to clear it of what she'd just seen. Her hand shot to clutch her necklace, a pendant gifted to her by her grandmother.

Before she could even run to the edge, a voice cut through her shock. "She isn't real. Just a phantom." The quiet voice intruded on her terror.

She glanced over her shoulder. A handsome man in his mid-thirties dressed as a gardener approached, carrying a pair of huge shears. The sight was so unexpected after what she'd just witnessed that she wasn't quite sure how to react. Brown eyes studied her with a mixture of pity and concern.

"What did you say?"

The man sighed, set his shears down, leaning them against his knee while he rubbed his palms on his brown work pants. "What you saw there, was the lady in white. She's haunted these cliffs since her death."

Her death? The woman she'd just seen was a…ghost?

"You believe in ghosts?" Jane turned her face once more to the cliffs.

The gardener turned his head toward the sea, his eyes focusing on something from the past. "I believe that evil leaves its mark on a place. Burns itself in the stones so deep that only something truly pure and good can get it out. These old stones have so much evil buried in them, I doubt the castle will ever rest. It isn't safe here, not for you." The gardener bent to pick up his shears again. "You should go, return to wherever you've come from, and forget this place."

She swallowed, a metallic taste still thick in her throat, focusing back on the gardener. "How often have you seen her? The lady in white?" Even as she spoke, the image of the woman's face flashed across her mind, and a chill swept through her entire body. She rubbed her hands over her arms.

He shrugged, eyes facing the cliffs as he answered, "She appears there on the cliffs whenever her kin return home."

She looked toward the hall, trying to bury the memory of sorrow and fear on the ghost's face. Anyone else might have been panicking after having just seen what she'd seen. But the nightly visions plaguing her had slowly forced her to accept that there were things beyond her explanation. Like ghosts.

"So the earl is here?" The earl was in residence. This was good news. She had been a little worried that he might be monitoring the estate from London.

"Yes. Arrived seven months ago. Been trying to restore the place. Not much good will it do. The ghosts are stirring again. He's upset the balance."

"The balance?" A sense of warning niggled at the back of her head, but she forced herself to ignore it—and to ignore the sense that she was losing her mind.

The gardener appeared to really see her for the first time. "The balance. Between the evil and the good. Evil rules the castle. Stalks the halls and torments those who dare to live inside."

Icy fingers raked down Jane's back.

"Is Lord Weymouth in danger? Being in the house?" It only occurred to her after she asked that the gardener might be right, and *she* might be in danger, too.

The gardener looked out to sea, his eyes dark. "I don't know. But if you plan to stay here, watch yourself, miss. Evil isn't always what you'd expect. It can take many forms." His voice dropped. "Many forms."

He turned and walked away. The momentary comfort his presence provided her vanished as she gazed upon his retreating form.

She wanted to know what he meant, but she doubted she'd get much more from him. She turned her attention back to the castle. The high windows reflected the sunlight as it started to peek out from the clouds.

The image of the lady in white flashed through her mind again, blinding her to the present for a brief instant. Her heart clenched in sadness, and fear rippled through her in tiny little waves, enough to keep her on edge. Had she witnessed a true apparition, or had her own imagination run away with her? She'd half hoped her dreams of being pushed from the cliffs had been only nightmares, yet that woman looked so familiar.

She had always believed in supernatural things. She was no longer a practicing Catholic in the churchgoing sense, but her faith was strong enough that she respected the truth that there were things in this world she couldn't understand. Like ghosts. And now she was going to enter a place bleeding with evil. She reached up to clutch the medallion of the archangel Michael that hung around her neck. The metal was warm from lying against her skin. It was a small comfort in the face of the looming castle and the fears of what might lurk in its shadows.

Chapter Two

He was cursed. There was no other explanation for it. Bastian Weymouth glared at the expensive toilet in his bathroom. Arms crossed over his chest, he shot a glance at the portly plumber who quivered in the doorway.

"What has you so agitated? I see nothing wrong." Bastian studied the room again, searching for signs of the disaster that the plumber insisted had taken place just a few minutes before he'd run to find Bastian.

The plumber gulped and took a deep breath. "The toilet was in place, and I was just tightening the pipes when the water exploded out of the bowl. It flooded the whole room!" The plumber waved his wrench about.

Bastian's displeasure deepened. The room wasn't wet. There wasn't one drop of water outside the bowl to confirm the plumber's story.

"I swear on my life, my lord! Water up to my ankles." The plumber jabbed at his pants where it showed the fabric soaked clear through up to his calves.

Yet the entire room was completely dry, and the plumber

had only fetched him a moment ago to explain the flooding. Flooding, which by all appearances, hadn't ever occurred.

It was just one more irritation in a long line of complications that had occurred during the renovations, which began when he'd moved back to Weymouth and Stormclyffe seven months ago, after his family's fifty-year absence. Leaky roofs, windowpanes shattering just hours after being installed, birds finding their way inside and dying when they broke their necks against the walls trying to escape. There were even workers talking about seeing a woman in a white dress along the cliffs. He'd never seen anything like that here. It was utter nonsense, but the list went on from there, each thing more frustrating than the last. All of it worsened the superstitions of the locals, especially the ones he had hired to repair everything. If he could just get the repairs completed, all of the superstitious nonsense would have to stop. The mutterings of "cursed" as he walked past local shops in the town would have to stop, too. He was tired of the black label his family bore in Weymouth because of the tragedies in their ancestral past. Restoring Stormclyffe, fixing it was the key. Something deep inside him compelled him to save the Hall. It was an almost tangible need to see the broken glass panes of the windows mended, the rooms dusted, and the broken stones replaced. Maybe returning the Hall to its former glory would make it look less like a tourist attraction for ghost hunters, and would make the townspeople stop spreading tales about it Then he might have a chance at a somewhat normal life, rather than be the target of village gossip.

His grandmother had been convinced that if he could fix Stormclyffe, there would be no more problems, no more tragedies, no more lost loved ones, like his father.

"It is fine, Mr. Tibbs. I'll compensate you for your services. I trust you'll stay here to see to the remaining water closets?"

"Thank you, my lord, but I have to say I don't feel

comfortable staying here after dusk." The portly man shifted on his feet, eyes darting around the lavish bathroom. "I'll return first thing in the morning."

Bastian didn't blame him. It was obvious Tibbs was a superstitious sort, and given the bloody history of Stormclyffe...well, that wasn't a surprise. Bastian's newly married grandparents had fled the castle in 1962 after an upstairs maid was found hanging from the rafters of the great hall. And they hadn't been the first to leave over the Hall's last two centuries.

The authorities hadn't been able to figure out how the girl had gotten out to the center beam to hang herself; there was no way it could be reached without an impossibly tall ladder. Yet the maid had been discovered swinging all the same. Nessy Harper, the victim, had been a local girl, and his family's reputation with the nearby town had been blackened. The coroner's report had read suicide, but there had been talk about his grandfather driving Nessy to it in some sort of doomed love affair. Bastian knew it was nonsense, but it didn't make the sting to his family's honor and pride any less significant.

Bastian's grandmother, who'd spent her last days in their London town house, had died murmuring about Nessy. He grimaced at the memory of her last moments when he'd been alone with her.

"Beware the shadows Bastian...they hold evil. Stay away from the castle. Poor sweet Nessy, milk-white eyes...she was so scared... Touch not the heart of evil... What once was broken must be mended." The frail old woman exhaled, and six-year-old Bastian had screamed. Her words had never made sense, but he'd always wondered if she'd meant that the castle shouldn't lay empty and crumbling. His grandparents had been the last heirs to live in the castle after all, and the guilt of leaving it behind might have weighed upon her in her final

hours. Many people suffered from delusions and superstitions in their twilight years.

"Tibbs, I'll pay triple your price if you get this toilet up and running before sunset."

The plumber's eyes bugged out in surprise. He nodded and rushed off to collect more tools.

Bastian left the water closet and headed back downstairs, ignoring the chaos of repair people and staff he'd hired to help with the upkeep of the castle.

"My lord," his butler, Randolph, announced. "The stone mason has finished repairing his work on the bell tower, but he said to advise you that if you wish to have the bell working properly you'll need to replace the clappers since all of the bells are missing them."

"Fine. I'll add it to the list of things I need to fix."

When Bastian turned to leave, his butler coughed politely. "One more thing, my lord. You have a visitor. I put her in the red drawing room."

Bastian cocked an eyebrow and scowled. "A visitor?" That was the last thing he needed.

Randolph swallowed, his eyes shifting away. "Er, yes. She said she is here to do research on the house, and you invited her in a letter. She's American."

American? For a second he couldn't imagine who Randolph was talking about. When the butler handed him the letter in question, obviously taken from the visitor, he studied it.

"Er…Yes. I remember." He scanned the note he'd hastily written several months ago. It all came back, the numerous e-mails and phone calls from the American woman named Jane Seyton. He'd asked her to wait until renovations were complete before she visited, yet here she was, showing up in the middle of numerous disasters. He'd made it abundantly clear she wasn't allowed any access to his family's archives.

Apparently Americans didn't understand blunt honesty. No surprise. He crumpled the letter in his fist, failing to quell the sudden frustration.

As if superstitious workmen weren't enough to cause him trouble, having the American here would prove to be one more irritation. She would have to be supervised to make sure she didn't pry into his family's documents and that nothing was taken intentionally from the house.

Randolph cleared his throat. "Will she be staying here, my lord? I can have a room prepared immediately."

Stay here? Surely he couldn't let the woman stay in the castle. Bastian was about to declare as much when something out of the corner of his eye flickered. A shadow at the edge of his vision seemed to be creeping along the wall toward him. He turned and focused in the direction he'd glimpsed it, but all signs of the shadow were gone.

I'm seeing things, too, blast it! These workmen are driving me to madness as well. He rubbed his eyes with his thumb and forefinger.

"My lord?" Randolph prompted, which made Bastian realize he must have been silent for several moments. The shadows had him on edge. Perhaps it would be nice to have a bit of company, if only she wasn't a bloody American. Given the rumors of ghosts and other such childish stories, most of the staff at Stormclyffe refused to stay overnight. Only Randolph and a few of the loyal staff from London remained after dark.

"I shall meet with her. She will not be staying here."

Jane Seyton was sure to be like every other historian he'd met and probably as stubborn as one of the Queen's corgis with a bone. Given half the chance, she'd run off to the nearest garden and bury his secrets where only she could find them. He didn't like anyone having that power over him.

Well, he did have a way with women. If she proved too

troublesome in getting her to leave, he'd simply seduce her. There wasn't a woman born yet that would say no to an invitation to dinner if the Earl of Weymouth asked her. No doubt she was a lonely little bookworm, probably wearing spectacles and never been kissed. The idea was almost charming. He smirked as he headed toward the drawing room. If he wanted her gone by nightfall, she'd be gone and all it would cost him was dinner.

When he reached the drawing room and laid a palm on the heavy oak door, it swung open revealing the rich red- and gold-papered walls and dust covered furniture. He hadn't had the chance to visit every room in the castle in the last seven months, since he'd been here sparingly, and he had definitely not been into this one. Randolph had been overseeing the cleanup of the rooms upon Bastian's instructions and given the number of rooms, many had yet to be opened.

Personally, he had been avoiding this room because it was the only room in the castle where a portrait of Isabelle hung. His grandmother had said looking upon Isabelle's face was bad luck, and since Stormclyffe had been abandoned for longer than he'd been alive, he'd never had the chance to find out himself if it was true. But now, seeing his ancestor for the first time…he was arrested at the sight.

There on the wall was the infamous woman whose swan dive off the cliffs had tainted his family's lives forever. Bastian studied the portrait for a moment. A fair-skinned woman with a hint of rose in her cheeks gazed out from the layers of oil with serious gray eyes. Her pale blue gown molded to her curves, and waves of rich ebony hair tumbled down her shoulders to tease the tops of her breasts. There was a curious expression on her face. She was happy, but wariness lurked in the depths of her eyes, as though she expected to lose her joy at any moment.

Below the painting, a flesh-and-blood woman stood with

her back to him. Windblown hair, dark as a raven's wing, spiraled down her back in enticing waves. He had the sudden urge to thread his fingers through the silken strands and shape her full curves with his other hand. A curious burning settled deep in his bones, and a ringing filled his ears as visions of him pinning her to a bed filled his mind. Wild, erotic thoughts tumbled through him, stealing his breath before he regained control and focused on his visitor again.

As though she'd heard his lustful thoughts, the woman turned to face him, cheeks flaming. She couldn't have known what he was thinking. His hand dropped from the door handle, and his jaw slackened in shock.

The dreamy gray eyes fixed on him were identical to the eyes of the woman painted above her. Noble, high cheekbones, curving brows, a sensual mouth made for kisses, and that nose, both delicate and impish, a perfect fit for the face of the woman before him. Her inky-black tresses and curves designed perfectly for a man's hands made her a living memory of a woman centuries gone.

Dear God… He repeated the words in his head over and over, mesmerized by the closeness of their shared features.

"You must be Lord Weymouth. I'm Jane Seyton."

The woman strode over to him, hand outstretched. Without thinking, he took it. Heat flared between them. He inhaled sharply.

She dropped his hand and retreated a step, her eyes wide. Had she felt the same jolt he had?

"I sent you a letter explaining that there couldn't be visitors here until renovations were complete. I also told you that I wouldn't let you see any of my family's documents." He grunted, but his gaze kept straying to the portrait behind her, comparing her features to Isabelle's. There was no obvious difference, and that alone had him blinking.

"I waited four months. I assumed the renovations were

complete…" Her gaze darted around the room, and she seemed to hesitate as though mentally kicking herself for believing the work would be done so soon. "If you'd only let me see the documents, I could be out of here in a week at most, I swear. I just need enough to be able to write a publishable thesis."

For some reason, her reaction angered him. He didn't want her here when the castle wasn't looking as it should. It was a reflection of him and his family, and to have her intrude was strange, even unsettling. A rush of temper overcame him—one he didn't know he could possess. The powerful emotion was almost foreign, as though not entirely his own.

"Are all of you Americans like this? Barge into a man's home, seeking evidence of scandals that ruined his family for two centuries? Have you no thought to how that destroys my family's fragile reputation?" he growled low through clenched teeth.

Her lips thinned, and the color in her cheeks faded. She looked pale, vulnerable, as though his outburst had upset her.

Her lovely eyes disappeared from his view as her gaze dropped to the floor. "I'm so sorry. I didn't realize it would be such an inconvenience." She sounded genuinely apologetic.

With a heavy sigh, he let his tense shoulders drop. "I apologize for my harsh reply, Miss Seyton. But really, you must leave. I am having trouble with the workmen, and we keep running into problems."

Her face brightened, gray eyes sparkling with energy again. "I need this, Lord Weymouth. If I can't find primary sources to accompany my assertions on the effect of the tragedies of Stormclyffe on the Weymouth community, my committee chair won't approve of my paper, and I'd have to start over on a totally new topic. I wouldn't be in your way. I'll stick to the libraries, the attics. That sort of thing. I could help you, if you like. I'm handy at quite a few things, not just research."

An odd stirring deep in Bastian turned his irritation at her into something different so quickly he barely had time to acknowledge it.

Desire.

Caught in slow-building currents of fascination and hunger for this complete and total stranger, he wanted to see if her handiness extended to activities between the sheets. She seemed to glow with a repressed sexuality, a woman unaware of her appeal. This was not the bookish woman he'd expected. Whatever he'd envisioned she would be like, perhaps wearing a tweed dress suit, spectacles perched on her nose, and a prim chignon, she was certainly not that.

There was something natural about her that appealed to him. She wore no makeup, and she was lovelier for it. Her somewhat casual attire looked comfortable, yet sophisticated. Quite unlike any of the women he had dated in the past. She was a woman who wouldn't wear a slinky dress and strappy high heels. Her sensuality was the sort that would flower before him when he had her naked on a bed.

What an image that was!

It took every ounce of his willpower to convince his body that a physical response was not a good idea. He closed the door and leaned back against it, examining her face, trying desperately to focus on it and not the rest of her body.

"Why do you care so much about the history of this place? I know from your letters you've never been here before. Why Stormclyffe? Why the obsession over people who are dead and gone? You can't change the past." In that brief instant, Bastian wondered who he was trying to convince: himself or her. He didn't know.

She turned away, moving about the room. She paused to pick up a framed photograph of his grandparents. Dust from the shelf, disturbed by her movement, wove through the streaks of sunlight coming in from the windows.

"There's something about Stormclyffe. It calls to me." Another blush highlighted her face, accenting her lovely cheeks. "I want to learn everything about it and uncover its secrets. You have to let me stay. *Please*."

He snatched a photograph out of her hand, clutching it to his chest with one palm. "Ms. Seyton."

"Jane."

It disturbed him. He couldn't get a read on this woman, couldn't decide why she was so interested in his home. It was obvious that her desire to stay wasn't just out of a scholarly interest. There was something more there, but she wouldn't tell him…yet.

He set the photograph aside on a shelf above her reach.

"What secrets do you think lurk in my home, *Jane*?" His voice caressed her name, hoping his silky tone would crumble her defenses a little. He had to regain command of the situation.

She nibbled her bottom lip, and a wave of arousal slammed into him like a freight train. A thousand delicious thoughts flashed through his head of what he'd like to do to those lips. He practically had to shake his head to clear it of the growing lust. What was wrong with him? He'd never been so out of control before. No better than a young man with his first girl, he couldn't keep his thoughts away from her and her body.

"Well?" He had the sudden desire to corner her, catch her, claim her. It had been ages since the predatory urge to seduce a woman had overtaken him. Bastian fought off his rising desire to unravel the puzzle she presented. Who was Jane Seyton? Sexy, yet innocent graduate student, or was she Mata Hari determined to seduce his secrets out of him for her own gain?

She pirouetted on her toe with all the grace of a ballerina

and followed the line of bookshelves, one finger leaving a line in the dusty wood near the faded spines of the books.

"Jane," he growled and cornered her at the end of the left side of the drawing room.

"Hmm?" She spun to face him, eyes widening at him as he glared down at her. She was short, and he towered over her by a good eight inches.

His voice dropped from a growl to a husky whisper. "My family's history is an unhappy one, and it is crucial I maintain what little dignity the dead have left. I need to know why you want to dig up the past. And don't feed me any stories about your dissertation. I know there's another reason you are here."

When she opened her mouth to protest, he placed his finger over her lips. They weren't pouty or full like most women he considered beautiful, but rather were a pale pink and petal soft. Lust exploded through him, an inferno of heat and insanity a coiled whip, striking his body, screaming for release. Again that sense of being controlled, as though a foreign entity had taken him over. He continued to touch her mouth.

He rubbed his thumb over her bottom lip, imagining his tongue licking it before sliding inside. "I can't have you underfoot, writing your ghost stories, unless you can give me a bloody good reason to let you. And I *hate* ghost stories." He wanted to pin her against the wall and kiss her until she couldn't remember her name. The thought was so out of place, so unexpected.

How was it possible to know that if he were to kiss just beneath the delicate line of her jaw, she would purr like a kitten? Or if he were to rock his hips into hers that she would arch her back and demand a kiss so deep they both would be gasping for air? It should have worried him that he knew just what to do to please her, but he was too lost in this moment, this heady rush of need and fire for her.

Her eyes, like the turbulent seas, flashed in ire.

A pinprick of light just behind her head burst into view, glowing and pulsing like an icy heart. He tore his eyes from Jane's face and stared in shock at the light as it grew. His lips parted, but it shot straight at him before he could make a sound. The light engulfed him and something rammed into him, rippled through his limbs, and took control.

He became a visitor in his own body, forced to watch from a distance, only feeling and seeing what the thing inside him wished him to experience. Fighting for a long moment against his loss of control, he finally surrendered, and the thing within took over fully, drawing him in, merging his consciousness with some unknown being.

"Isabelle!" A hoarse cry tore from his lips, yet the voice wasn't his.

There was no stopping it. A harsh passion seized him, and he pulled her body tight to his, pinning her wrists at her sides as he took her mouth. He trapped her between himself and the bookcase, reveling in her squeak of surprise.

In a frenzy, he explored her plush curves, his hands shaping and stroking every bit of her he could touch. It had been years, so many years since he'd touched her, his sweet Isabelle. She nipped his chin, her hands curling around his shoulders, digging in to drag him closer as she yielded to his dominance.

A roaring wind filled his ears, drowned out the thundering of his blood and the drumbeat of his heart. Glimpses between kisses revealed sharp electric-blue spheres flaming like distant stars in the small black pupils of her eyes. She was there, beyond his reach, yet in his arms. How was this possible? He'd been trapped in the walls for nearly two centuries, unable to find her or hold her.

My beloved. Isabelle.

He groaned and released her wrists to cup her lush,

rounded bottom, lifting her against him, clenching hard as he rocked his aching cock against her heated center.

He rammed hard, driving himself against her, no matter that clothes separated him from his desire. She cried out against his ear, the sound a symphony of pleasure that snapped and cracked between them like flames devouring wood.

It was madness to want her, madness to need a stranger. He knew the body wasn't truly his Isabelle's but he could feel her inside it, trying to reach out to him.

But he did know her; something deep within him roared in defiance, as though his soul knew hers, even if his mind did not.

Must punish her. Must prove she cannot live without me.

"Why did you leave me? Why did you jump?" he demanded.

She shook her head, eyes wild and suddenly bright with fear.

He snarled against her lips and kissed her harder, one hand unbuttoning her trousers to loosen them, before sliding his hand beneath the waist of her pants to cup her arse. His fingers dipped between her thighs, finding wet heat. She moaned something unintelligible and shifted closer to him, urging him on with her body when words failed her. Her mouth met his with an equal fire and heady lust, just as she writhed against him, trying to satisfy her needs.

Surrender to me, love. Ease this ache of mine, my broken heart.

He tore his lips from hers and nibbled a path down her neck, savoring the faintly salty-sweet taste of her skin beneath his tongue.

His fingers stroked her entrance again and again until she shuddered and convulsed. He sank his teeth into her neck, hoping the love bite was hard enough to leave a mark so others would know she was his. For however long he possessed this body, for however long Isabelle was in his arms, he had to lay his claim to her. He pulled his hand out from between her thighs and wrapped his arms around her back, clutching her to him. How long would he have to hold her before he lost her again? He could feel his control of the body slipping...slipping away. Despair snuffed out his lust, and a chill surged through him. With a cry of rage and agony, he was torn from the body and forced back into the stones of Stormclyffe.

Freezing pain tore through Bastian, and his knees buckled. The foreign presence, that sense of someone else within him was gone. He went down like a stone, hitting the carpet. His eyelids fell shut. His breaths coming in soft pants were the only steady thing in him. The rest of him vibrated with energy, tiny electric shocks pulsing through his body.

After an eternity, the fog in his head seemed to clear. Every muscle in his body screamed in protest as he sat up. A body lay next to him, facedown on the floor. A woman...the American. It all came rushing back. The passion, the fire, and the fact that he hadn't been in control of himself. He'd done things to her, possibly without her permission. And the name Isabelle still hung on his lips as though he had screamed it until he lost his voice.

What in God's name had happened? There was no rational explanation for what had just occurred. Knowing this made him shudder so harshly that his bones seemed to crack.

"Ms. Seyton—Jane..." He shook her awake.

She murmured groggily and rolled over onto her back.

"What the hell happened?" Her muttered curse was oddly reassuring. "Were we kissing?" She touched her kiss-swollen lips and then her eyes flicked to his. "Oh my God. I swear I don't do this."

"I don't either..." He frowned and rubbed the back of his neck, trying to dispel the guilt at not being able to explain his actions. He'd kissed plenty of women, but never in such circumstances as these. It was as if he'd been...possessed. If such a thing could actually occur. Which it couldn't. "I'm sorry for whatever I might have…er…done to you without your consent."

He glanced down at his groin, worried at the sight of his erection. Why was his body not responding to his mind's wishes? There shouldn't be arousal, fire, passion. Yet all three of these were rioting through him making it perfectly clear his body still wanted to bed the woman sitting next to him. His gaze raked her, taking in the sight of her flushed cheeks, swollen lips…and teeth marks between her neck and shoulder.

"I remember going along with it and liking it, but I sort of felt like there was no control." She dragged her fingers through the tangle of black locks, and her gaze slid away, her cheeks pink as her fingers fumbled with the loose buttons of her jeans, securing them back in place.

Bastian felt like a damned fool. He'd just snogged a woman in his drawing room without any control over himself. If he were a man who believed in ghosts, he might think that his ancestor Richard had taken over his body. Possessed him. But that was *impossible*.

Bastian shrugged it off as nerves. He refused to let himself believe anything else. The castle renovations were getting to him. Maybe he was having some sort of psychotic breakdown from the stress.

Yes. That made sense. He was having a mental breakdown.

Jane got to her feet and held out a hand to him. He accepted, letting her pull him up and got a better look at her.

She wore jeans that hugged her shapely body and a thick gray sweater like she was ready to climb aboard his sailboat and float out on the tide with him. Again he was surprised that her natural beauty was such an allure to him. After years of polished, posh princesses, it was strange that a woman like this commanded his attention.

He was hardly a romantic. He'd never seen the need to

fall in love or get involved in any messy entanglements of the heart. He took women, gave them pleasure, and sated his own needs. The romance of red roses and chocolates weren't for men like him. There was no need to buy appreciation from his women, nor did he particularly feel the need to reward them for succumbing to their passions in his arms. He preferred straining naked bodies in sweaty sheets to poetry and dinners for two. Sex was akin to business transactions, and although Bastian knew he viewed it coldly, he enjoyed it. He didn't need any of the emotional intimacy or love that many women seemed to think was required. And he'd never stopped to consider why that was.

But the idea of taking his time, savoring Jane's taste and inhaling the faint scent of her wild-orchid perfume while he claimed her, was incredibly tempting.

"Why are you looking at me like that? Isn't it enough that you mauled me like a wild bear?" She shoved him; her palm made contact with his chest, and he tensed with heat and need. Although upon first meeting her he expected her to be a timid little nose-in-her-book scholar type, she wasn't. Her politeness gave way to an intimacy that confused him. She wasn't exactly treating him the way others did, with respect and awe. No…she had just shoved him like she would a brother or perhaps a lover, or at the least someone she was comfortable with. Why had she done that?

Strangely, he realized her rough-and-tumble action fascinated him. Her sensual playfulness was incredibly erotic. None of the previous women he'd been with had ever been playful. They'd been coy and aggressive, but never teasing. He had to admit he liked it. A woman like her, with full curves and strength just ached to be taken hard, ravaged to within an inch of dying from too much pleasure.

He bit his lip so hard blood beaded, and he licked it away. If he didn't get inside Jane soon, pound into her sweet heat until she screamed he'd... Bastian wrenched control of his body back from that deep inner specter that seemed determined to pin her to the floor and spread her thighs. She was turning him inside out with desire. He hadn't wanted a woman this bad in a long time.

With every last ounce of willpower, he assumed the mantle of his British upbringing and scrounged deep down for the last bit of his manners. "I apologize profusely for my actions. I have no idea what came over me." And he meant it. How could he begin to explain what had just come over him?

She didn't reply, so he studied her for a long moment, those piercing eyes of hers cut straight through to his core. He couldn't help but wonder...she had kissed him back. She hadn't tried to push him away or fight him when he'd kissed her. Why?

"You have no idea why you kissed me?" Her tone sounded odd, as though she might know the answer to her own question.

He shrugged, completely at a loss to explain himself. "I haven't the slightest idea. I suppose it's all the stress from the renovations. I've had headaches for days now, and this is probably one more way my body is reacting. You see now why it's in your best interest to leave my house. I wouldn't want you to remain here when things could get...complicated." He placed a palm on the small of her back, ushering her to the door.

She twirled around, escaping his touch so she could go back and retrieve her briefcase and purse.

"Actually, I don't mind complicated. Perhaps my being here will help reduce the stress."

It took all of his control not to reply that the best de-stressing he could use was her on a bed beneath him.

"Miss Seyton, you cannot stay." He looped his arm through hers, attempting to drag her, albeit politely, toward the door.

She dug in her heels and wedged herself into the doorway. "Wait! Please! *What once was broken must be mended.*" Her words were expelled in a breathless rush and he froze.

"What did you say?"

Her face darkened as she met his stare. "What once was broken must be mended."

"Where did you hear that?" He whirled her around, pinning her by her shoulders against the doorjamb.

"I…I don't know," she whispered. Her body trembled beneath his hands. "I can't explain it. It's like the words were on the tip of my tongue and when you tried to make me leave…they just rushed out."

His grandmother's warning. The need to fix his ancestral home. This woman who could be Isabelle's twin. It was as though puzzle pieces were sliding into place, but Bastian didn't want to see the puzzle. He didn't want to face this, whatever it was. He might lose more than he already had. Stormclyffe had taken his father, destroyed his grandfather's life, and countless other generations going back two hundred years. Anyone staying here was at risk. If Jane stayed, she would be at risk, too.

"Let me stay. Please." Her begging undid the cold knot inside his chest.

Perhaps if he let her use the library, just for a short while, he could ply her with reasons the curse didn't exist and then send her on her way. If he was very lucky, he might stop her writing her thesis all together, so no one would come here in search of ghosts.

"If, and I do mean, *if* I allow you to stay, you will not be permitted to review documents unless I have approved them first. You will go nowhere in this castle unless I have given express permission. I will give you one week. That is all. You will not disrupt me, nor the workmen, nor cause any kind of disturbance. Do you understand?"

She was already nodding eagerly before he'd even asked the last question.

A heavy sigh escaped his lips. "Very well. Then you may stay. But if at any point in time, I feel you are underfoot, I will have you leave, and you will brook no argument."

"Deal." She held out her hand.

He released his grip on her shoulders but didn't shake her hand. Touching her once had led to violent passions. He would not be so foolish as to touch her again.

"Sorry," she muttered, dropping her hand.

For a moment they just stared at each other, neither of them speaking. He'd never felt so awkward in his life, but something about Jane ruffled his feathers.

She'd broken the spell of tension with a shrug and produced a notebook and pen, flipping to an empty page and started to scrawl notes. "So this has happened often?"

He purposely gave her a blank look, hoping it would dissuade her from further questions.

She continued. "The attempted seduction of visiting ladies?"

He rolled his eyes. What was he to do with this irritating and completely beguiling creature?

"Have you not been listening? There are no visiting ladies. You are the first official guest Stormclyffe has had in half a century. I only started renovations seven months ago and moved in a few months ago." He ushered her down a hallway, trying to remind himself where the library was. It would be a safe place to put her while he saw to his duties. No doubt she could lose herself in the books for hours, and he could check on her later. It would give him time to secure his more private papers in his office, away from her prying eyes. Even though he'd reluctantly agreed to let her stay, it didn't mean he had to provide her with any real substantial research material.

"So you didn't bring anyone with you? A girlfriend I mean?" Her blunt question caught him off guard, and he stumbled a step.

"What? No...I am not involved with anyone at the moment. I'm not one for getting involved at all really. In fact, I plan never to marry." Where that honesty came from, he didn't know, but he wanted her to hear it. Maybe that would make her understand what sort of man he was. One who didn't date women with designs on becoming the next Countess of Weymouth.

She raised a brow as they continued to walk down the long corridor. Much of the castle's exterior was stonework, but a good majority of the inside had been rebuilt to have a more modern design, well, modern enough at any rate. Bastian knew that most of the interior of the Hall was a combination of Regency and Georgian styles. Richard had been the last of his ancestors to make major changes to the architecture and design on the inside as well as select the furnishings.

She was still gazing at him somewhat reproachfully. "What's that look for?" he asked.

"Isn't there supposed to be an heir and a spare or something? You're an earl. Isn't that part of your heritage? Continue the family line and everything?"

He chuckled, the sound dark and almost unnatural, startling even himself. "I'm not sure my family line should be continued, given our history. Perhaps it's best if the line dies out with me."

She wrinkled her nose. "Then why fix the castle? Why bother if you don't plan to share the success of restoring your home with a family and making it last for generations to come."

"Damnation!" He halted and smacked a balled fist into his opposite palm. "Even if I'm the last, it doesn't mean what I'm doing is irrelevant. I don't plan to marry, but that doesn't mean I won't give my life purpose by rebuilding my family's ancestral home." Hadn't she herself whispered the words? *What once was broken must be mended?* The Hall was broken by grief, by tragedy, by loss. It wasn't just the stones, but if he started there, he might heal his family's wound. A meager hope, one he clung to without any real hope it would work. But what else could he do? Even if he never set foot in the Hall again, he feared the curse would cling to him and destroy anything he cared about. Better to be here alone and try to fix the place. He had to finish what his father started.

"I'm sorry. I didn't mean to offend you. I was just making an observation." She combed one hand through her hair, tugging it away from her face.

Bastian wasn't sure what he should have said in response to her apology and was grateful that the library door was a few feet away. After what had just happened, he needed some time to escape her and regain his composure and his control. The violent mood swings he had just experienced in the last few minutes were entirely unlike him, and he suspected her presence was at the root of their cause. Avoiding her at least temporarily might help him solve matters.

There wasn't much in the way of natural light in the castle, but Bastian's predecessors had installed modern lightning. A massive three-tiered chandelier hung in the great hall, crystals beading the cables that connected the tiers. The chandelier cast a muted light along the ceiling, the faint glow warming the room below. Cobwebs laced the corners of the halls, out of reach of even the most agile maids. The space between the rafters and the floor beneath their feet was filled with cold air.

"Bastian, this is where the maid died, right? In 1962?"

He froze, shoulders tensing, before he looked over at her. While the papers had published the news of the maid's mysterious death, no mention had been made nor pictures taken of the location of her body. How the bloody hell did this woman know where the maid had died? He raked a hand through his dark blond hair and scowled. "She was found hanging from the middle rafter." He pointed straight above them.

She craned her neck back, obviously considering the location of the beam. "How could she have gotten there? The beam isn't reachable from any place but the ground, and she would have needed a huge foot ladder. Don't you think it's odd?"

"It wasn't a suicide." His voice was harder than stone. "My family believes someone killed her."

She stilled, going so silent, it was as if she forgot to breathe.

"So who did it?" She caught up with him as he started walking again.

His gaze flicked to hers, a pulse of heat shooting between them. She licked her lips unthinkingly, and his gaze followed the movement, and he felt to the need to draw a deeper breath. The sexual tension between them was thick enough that he could have sliced it with a blade. She kept pace with him as he kept walking until he paused at a pair of tall gilded doors.

"Here is the library. Please follow me." He moved ahead of her and opened the door. Her little gasp made him smile. If there was one place that would garner such a reaction, it would be the library of Stormclyffe Hall.

"I've never…it's so…" Words seemed to fail her.

He laughed, genuinely pleased at her reaction. He had struck the little American speechless at least for the moment.

"This way, I'll take you to the family archives." Once more he had his hand on her lower back and guided her toward the documents, which would distract her for the rest of the day.

He hoped.

Chapter Three

A kiss. A tangle of limbs, melding mouths, and a climax that had ripped her apart inside. It had changed her from the inside out. Jane rested her fingertips on her lips, falling deep into the hazy memory of their fiery passion.

It hadn't been a daydream. One minute they'd been talking and the next… Something had taken her over, and like a stranger in her own body, she'd flung herself at Bastian and kissed him—more than kissed him. He'd had his hand between her legs, and he had made her come. It was wild, insane, and erotic. It was also disturbing. If she hadn't known better, she might have thought she'd been possessed. When they were together, there was this electric charge that seemed to twine about them, tugging them closer and closer until they shared the same breath, the same heartbeat. Kissing Bastian had been natural and right, even though she'd never met him before in her life.

She had tried to act like what happened meant nothing, that some temporary passion had swept them both away, but she couldn't shake that feeling of sharing her body and losing control to someone else. And even more frighteningly, she couldn't erase the memory of her lips forming one name over and over as she came apart in his arms.

Richard.

Had the stories of this place gotten to her? Was she going mad from the stress of her dissertation and the desire to end the bizarre and nightmarish dreams that haunted her almost nightly? Those seemed like more plausible explanations, but she couldn't dismiss the sense that the answers to what was happening here and to her were just within reach. As though veiled by a cloud of mist, she couldn't make out the shapes clearly. Solutions and answers were buried deep in the mire and fog.

As she trailed behind Bastian, she was torn between admiring his tight ass molded in charcoal slacks and admiring the beautiful interior of the castle. He hadn't prepared her for the library though. Nothing could have.

None of the photographs of the Hall had ever revealed the library's interior. She had assumed it was because it was like any other library in any other castle or manor house. How wrong she was.

The room was awash in bold reds and a range of pale yellows to deep golds. Wall panels were decorated with art that looked so familiar.

"Is this what I think it is?" She pointed to one of the panels with a red-painted background and a Chinese scene in yellow.

His lips twitched. "If you're thinking of William Alexander's book *Views of China*, then you are correct. Richard apparently enjoyed the text immensely and had an artist replicate many of the etchings."

She smiled. "I can see why. The culture and the life… Can you imagine what it must have been like for Alexander?" William Alexander had been an English watercolorist who visited China and made drawings of the scenery and life during his time there. His *Views of China* was a highly valued and much-admired work. Even the Brighton Pavilion Palace, which was built in Brighton for George, Prince of Wales as a seaside palace, boasted similar scenes inspired by Alexander's book.

Bastian's expression softened. "I would give so much to see through the eyes of the dead, to see what they have seen, to experience times I cannot fathom." He looked away then, his gaze roving the two-story-high shelves of the library, but Jane couldn't tear her attention from him.

How many women had fallen under his spell? A man haunted by his family's past, a dedicated scholar, and as brooding and captivating as Lord Byron. If she let her thoughts run away with her, she knew Bastian would distract her from her dissertation.

Focus, Jane, focus.

The last thing she needed was to fall for him. After Tim, her heart couldn't take it. She'd only just managed to stitch the bleeding, torn organ back together. Bastian would not be the one to tear it apart again.

They strolled farther into the room, and she tilted her head back to better admire the lotus-shaped chandeliers. Intricate paintings decorated each of the petals on every chandelier. In the middle of the wall to the right, a vast fireplace rose up with columns on either side, adorned with twining serpents. Unable to resist the urge, she hastened over to touch the pale Swedish green marble that formed the snake. The serpent's features had been sculpted so precisely that she half expected it to come to life and bite her.

A massive mirror hung above the fireplace, and it reflected the windows on the opposite side of the library. A lush landscaped garden seemed to stretch for miles beyond the fireplace. The deceptive placing of the mirror created an enchanting illusion that one could walk through the mirror into an alternate world. A marble dragon perched atop the mirror's gilt-edged frame. Its wings were spread wide, jaws gaping open as it silently roared.

She gasped. A sudden flash of something wild and fearful ripped through her an instant before it was gone.

"Jane?" Bastian placed a hand on her shoulder but then almost immediately he removed it and stepped back from her. "Are you well? You gave a little start just now."

She hastily nodded. "Yes, I'm fine. It's just…that dragon. It's so…" How could she describe having such a visceral reaction to a stone creature?

"Fierce. The beast is fierce." He crossed his arms over his chest, scowling back at the dragon.

She realized then she was still touching the serpent's head and pulled her hand away.

"Fierce indeed. I didn't expect such decorations in a library."

He chuckled. "The music room in the Pavilion in Brighton was modeled after Stormclyffe."

Ahh, I had guessed right then.

"My ancestor, Richard, believed something more… medieval would suit Stormclyffe. Our coat of arms bears a dragon after all. He designed the dragon to appear as you see them. The Pavilion's dragons are more complacent-looking, and merely hold the curtains in place."

The eyes of the dragon seemed to watch her as she shifted from one foot to the other. It's long, angular snout looked ready to spew fire and puff smoke from its nostrils. The way it hunched over the mirror gave her the distinct impression it wasn't merely guarding the library, but rather hunting the library's inhabitants. It was an unsettling thought.

"You don't like it?" The earl teased her.

She nibbled her lip thoughtfully. "It's not that I don't like it. I just feel like it's watching me."

He grinned. "Don't tell me you are afraid? Isn't your dissertation connected to mysteries and hauntings? That's what your letters stated. I didn't think you would be so foolish as to pick a topic that would frighten you."

Before she even had time to think, she'd socked him in the shoulder again. She'd punched an earl. This was a bad habit she was forming.

He merely caught her by the shoulders, stilling her when she would have retreated from him. Their faces were so close that she could see endless books reflected in his gaze. He moved one hand up to cup her chin.

"Perhaps," he murmured huskily, "you should have directed your dissertation to something less threatening."

Brimming with anger, she bit back a viperlike retort and smiled sweetly. "Such as?"

The wicked glint in his eyes warned her he was going to say something infuriating.

"Why not write about the effects of wildflowers in various English counties? Surely that would inspire no fears?"

"Wildflowers?" She knocked his hand away from her chin and turned her back on him. *Provoking man.* She didn't have much of a natural temper, but what little was there, he found and prodded repeatedly until she broke and snapped at him. Still, she probably should be thankful. She and Tim had never fought; he'd never irritated her. She couldn't fall for someone when they drove her crazy. Bastian's ability to annoy her was, therefore, a small blessing.

"Oh come now, Jane," he said her name so softly, almost a croon, the way a man would to soften his lover's injured pride. That only made her more upset. He thought he could work some seductive magic to sidetrack her in her quest for research. The man was a nuisance. Couldn't he just leave her to the books and get on with his day? Instead he insisted on dragging her around the castle and teasing her.

She didn't reply. Not yet. When he came up behind her and gently placed a hand on her shoulder, turning her body back to face his, she finally had to meet his stare.

"What's the matter?" he asked.

"What's the matter? I could ask you the same question. You're teasing me and yet you—" She didn't dare finish. It felt like he was flirting with her, but maybe she was wrong. The last thing she wanted for him to think was that she viewed herself worthy of his attentions or that she wanted them. It would only complicate things. While she didn't mind, as she'd insisted to him earlier, that had been under the pretense of being allowed to stay and conduct her research. She hadn't actually thought she'd start to succumb to his charms. It was a good thing he had the ability to infuriate her as well. That made him far less attractive.

"Can you please just take me to the records?"

"Of course." His tone was more reserved. The wall that had started to crumble between them was solid again. "This way."

He led her to a shelf near the floor on the other side of the fireplace where several tall tomes were behind a sheet of glass. He bent, pressed his fingertips to the panel, and slid the glass to the side, making the large books accessible.

"Here are the recorded histories and family trees of the Weymouth line. I won't allow you access to any private letters or other documents from my family. I assume three hundred years worth of information is enough to keep you occupied for the afternoon. I can guide to you other sources tomorrow." He paused, then leaned one shoulder against the bookshelves.

The man was hot when he leaned that way. Why did *leaning* have to be so damned sexy? Maybe it had to do with the way it called attention to the long, lithe shape of his legs and the muscles of his shoulders. She wanted to smack herself for even going there. She shouldn't be thinking about him like that. *Dissertation. Focus on your research.*

"That reminds me. Where are you staying? The trip to the town can be treacherous after dark. I wouldn't want you driving off the cliffs into the sea. I would prefer to have someone escort you back." He announced this casually but there was something odd in his expression, an emotion she couldn't read clearly.

Was he worried about her? She mentally shrugged it off. Of course he didn't care about her, not that way. After what had happened between them in the drawing room, she was hesitant to do anything that might give the wrong impression about her. He might not think of her at all in the way she was currently thinking about him. *Naked.* And how she'd like to get him out of those dark slacks and light gray sweater that molded to his broad chest muscles.

Bad idea. Must not think of him naked. She chastised herself. His offer probably stemmed from worries over a lawsuit from her family if she drove her rental car off the cliff and died.

"I've got a room booked at a little inn."

Bastian waved a hand. "Don't worry about that. Do your research this afternoon. I will drive you into town tonight around sunset."

"You'll drive me?" Weren't earls supposed to have chauffeurs?

"I do know how to drive." He flashed a mocking smile. "Even my ancestors drove their own sporting carriages. But to answer your question, my driver is still in London along with some of the other staff and won't move in until the restorations are complete. I've actually been driving myself since I moved back here."

He sounded smug, as if he'd proved false her accusation

that he couldn't operate a car. Had he taken her comment as an insult? God, she hoped not. She mentally kicked herself.

"Oh. Then yes, that would be fine."

"Excellent." He stepped away from the bookshelves. "I'll come to collect you later. Enjoy your research." He flashed her a cocky smile that did something funny to her knees before he took his leave and left her alone with the dragon and his hoard of jealously guarded books.

Jane removed the first of several volumes from the shelf and carried it to a nearby reading table. A cloud of dust billowed up as she set the book down on the polished cherrywood. The motes twirled and danced through the stray beams of light from the high windows. A heavy silence filled the library, almost tangible. Each movement Jane made elicited a loud sound: the whisk of paper as she removed it from her briefcase, the rapid *click* of her ballpoint pen as she pressed the cap with her thumb. She collected her materials and opened her notebook to a fresh page, hoping to dispel the eerie silence of the room by losing herself in the text on the pages before her.

She peeled back the heavy brown leather cover of the book. The first few pages were blank, but the third bore an elaborate sketch of a family tree. The names were inscribed with a quill pen, the ink faded to a pale brown but still legible. She carefully took notes and replicated the tree, which started with births and marriages in 1607.

For the next three hours, she remained in her chair, diligently recording the Weymouth earldom's history from the births to the deaths of its more prominent family members. Until Richard's death, the Weymouth line seemed normal in its deaths and births. After Richard's passing, the pattern changed showing an extraordinary amount of tragic deaths and accidents. There were people drowning at sea, falling from ladders in the orchards, and unexpected infant deaths. A majority of the victims were women who had married into the Stormclyffe family. There were many more gruesome deaths and more unexplained accidents or occurrences. Fires broke out in the castle several times, always starting in bedrooms where the women who married into the Weymouth family were sleeping. Crops on the estate failed for several years while the crops of the farmers from the surrounding areas thrived.

Maybe the rumors were right. The entire family seemed truly cursed.

She set her pen down and closed the large tome. It didn't seem to matter whether it was supernatural or merely bad lack—the facts didn't lie. Since Richard's bride jumped to her death in 1811, the family line and home had suffered through a nearly endless chronology of heartbreak.

The last entry in the record book stated a fact she hadn't known.

Bastian's father had died in a car accident at the age of forty-three. When she had investigated Bastian's background, she hadn't focused on his parents. She knew logically that since he was the current Earl of Weymouth, it meant his father must have passed away, but there were no records detailing how. Only Bastian and his mother survived. If Bastian stuck true to his words that he would never marry, that meant he wouldn't continue his family's line. The title would pass to distant cousins, but the direct line would perish.

She'd judged him too harshly, thinking him a fool for not wanting to marry. Now she wondered if he wouldn't commit to building a future with anyone because so many tragic and untimely deaths weighed the family tree down. Even if he refused to believe in the curse, perhaps somewhere deep in the recesses of his mind lay a fear of bringing another child into this world under the Weymouth title. Tears burned at the corners of her eyes. How devastating to believe, even subconsciously, that any baby he might have could be condemned to death by his family's curse. It would explain why he kept himself emotionally distant from others. His playboy reputation might make her blush, but the man himself was a still a mystery.

A muscle cramped in her neck. A series of small knots had formed after hours of her head bending over the desk. She pushed her research materials across the table and reached behind her to massage the area, soothing the tension away.

As far as her dissertation was concerned, she could use the chronology of deaths and disasters of the family to highlight its influence on myths and legends around this particular estate. She would work it into the stories connected to other estates around England. If she was able to talk Bastian into letting her photograph or perhaps scan the copies of the family tree with particular entries regarding some of the deaths of the family members, she would be able to cite them as primary sources.

The sun emerged from the clouds, causing long shadows to stretch along the carpeted floor. She watched their slow-moving progress for several minutes as the darkness consumed the patterned carpet. One shadow seemed to move more quickly than the others. It expanded rapidly, consuming the light on the table closest to the window. An identifiable shape began to form.

A dragon.

Her gaze shot up to the windows, and she expected to see a bird spreading its wings in a nearby tree, which would have explained the unusual shape. But there were no trees visible through the glass. The dragon shadow twisted its head, and its tail lashed out in a whip-like flash. Its wings spread wide, and for a brief second, she thought she could hear a distant roar and feel the library's floor quake beneath her.

She cried out and leaped from her chair, backing up until

she hit the bookcase behind her. Something crashed to the floor at her feet, but she dared not look. Her heart pounded against her ribs as she searched for the shadow, which seemed to have vanished as quickly as it had appeared.

As her breathing slowed, and the faint ringing in her ears faded, she glanced down and noticed a small leather-bound book on the floor. It was partially open over one of her feet. Bending down, she gingerly picked it up and studied it more closely. The pages were full, but not with printed text. Instead, each page was filled with scrawling handwriting, the archaic cursive style beautiful and half-faded. Dates were inscribed in the top left corner.

It was a diary.

Transfixed, she sank back into her seat and began to read. As she read, she could see it all unfold as though she were a visitor there, watching unseen like a ghost.

April 21st, 1810

I was pouring over the Hall's account books my steward had prepared for me. The task was wearisome but necessary. I longed to have a distraction, something that could take my mind off my concerns. Sir Lionel Huntington had written to say he would be visiting again this afternoon to discuss the future of his daughter, Cordelia. While I am ready to take a bride, I'm not sure she is the one for me. Sir Lionel was apparently determined to see his daughter become the Countess of Weymouth. The chit is pretty enough. Honey-blond hair and hazel eyes. But there is a coldness to Miss Huntington's demeanor and presence that unnerves me. What's more, her family bears a rather dark history, one that I fear I cannot completely overlook. They are descendents of a woman who was accused of witchcraft in Lancashire. She was proven innocent, but I cannot help but wonder still… Does darkness run through the veins of her female lineage? Sometimes I see Miss Huntington's eyes gleam in a way that makes me wonder and worry.

A light rap on my study door disturbed my thoughts.

"Enter," I called out.

My butler, Mr. Shrewsbury, poked his gray-haired head around the edge of the door.

"The new innkeeper, Mr. Braxton, is here to see you my lord. I have put him and his daughter in the red drawing room."

"Thank you, Shrewsbury." Relief poured through me.

Finally, an excuse to escape the accounts. I am interested in meeting Mr. Braxton. Since he is a new resident to the town, it is important that I meet with the man and establish good relations with him.

I pushed back my chair and stood, checking my appearance. My trousers were clean, my waistcoat unwrinkled, a veritable miracle given that I'd spent the last few hours slumped over my desk during my labors. With a hasty hand run through my hair, I was satisfied I looked suitable for company and headed toward the drawing room.

It is my favorite room, one full of light and color. It boasts of a fair amount of books and paintings of my family from years before. A pair of love seats face each other with a small table next to each where a tea tray could be placed for visitors. When I entered, I found Mr. Braxton perched on one of the two love seats. A maid set a tray of tea and biscuits on the table next to him.

"My lord!" Braxton got to his feet immediately, a genuine smile on his face. With ruddy cheeks and a muscled figure barely concealed by his tailored waistcoat, Braxton was a fit and amiable man.

"Welcome to my home, Mr. Braxton. I am delighted you were able to come and meet with me." I immediately sought out the man's daughter, expecting a plump, whey-faced creature. The woman stood in the far corner with her back to me as she

admired my books.

My first thought was how lovely her figure was. When she turned to face me, my heart stopped. The world came to an abrupt halt. I couldn't breathe. She was so beautiful, something deep in my chest began to hurt. There was a fire in her eyes and warmth in her smile. The blush in her cheeks was becoming, and the dark curls that framed her face accented her creamy skin. I was lost to her in that moment. I wondered if I could ever want another woman except her.

"My lord." Miss Braxton's voice was husky and a little breathless, as though she was reacting to me much in the same way I reacted to her. I hoped so. I did not wish to be the only one so completely affected.

"Miss Braxton, it is a pleasure." I strode up to her and bent over the hand she offered hesitantly. I pressed a kiss to her skin. The scent of rosewater filled my nose. The delicate perfume was a perfect accent to the woman who wore it.

"Thank you for extending an offer to visit." Mr. Braxton appeared at his daughter's side, reminding me that Miss Braxton and I were not alone, no matter how much I might wish we were.

"Of course. Please sit." I gestured to the settees, and we all took our seats.

I spent the next hour conversing with Braxton about Weymouth and how best to settle in with the local folk. Unlike many of the other inns in the county, Braxton's accommodations were of a higher quality, and many aristocrats would likely wish to stay at the new inn as they passed through on their way to the other parts of England. Despite the conversation distracting me, I managed to keep my eyes on Miss Braxton. I relished the way she kept glancing at my books with keen interest. I suspected she must be a lady who enjoyed reading and wasn't merely a fair-faced creature with no real thoughts in her head. Women with no interests and no intellectual pursuits held no appeal for me.

As the conversation came to its natural end, I bid my guests good-bye with the invitation for them to return on the morrow for dinner. As I watched Miss Braxton and her father depart, a piece of my soul seemed to separate from my body and accompany her home. I had never felt such a kindred spirit in anyone, man or woman. Come the morrow, I knew I would be desperate for a glimpse of her. Dinner could not come soon enough.

Chapter Four

Jane pulled herself out of the story in the journal. *Richard's journal.* This was an invaluable primary source. A direct account written in Richard's own hand. Maybe the true story to the tragedy lurked somewhere in these pages. She looked over at the inconspicuous location where the journal had been hiding between two boring collections of philosophical essays by long-forgotten authors. It was possible the diary had been there for years, and no one had noticed it. The book's spine was blank, and to a casual reader perusing books, it held no particular appeal or attraction. If Bastian ever found out his ancestor's handwritten account of his life was here, he'd probably lock it up and never let her see it. He had told her she wouldn't have access to the family's private papers. A family journal would most likely be considered private.

A little voice whispered dark thoughts in her head. *Take the journal. Put it in your bag and keep it just until you finish your research.*

With a guilty little flip of her heart, she hastily tucked the diary into her bag before she could she talk herself out of it. Her decision came not a moment too soon. The library door opened, and Bastian strode in. He'd changed into a pair of faded jeans, black boots, and a black T-shirt that showed off his muscular physique. He still wore the expensive watch she'd noted earlier, and his gold hair was messily coiffed as though he'd stepped out of a windy Ralph Lauren ad. She half expected a leggy blonde to show up and casually run her hands through his hair. He was a walking *GQ* cover.

The earl who wore jeans. She laughed without meaning to, and his gaze fell on her when he spotted her at the table.

"Something amusing?" He raised one eyebrow in a challenge. Did they teach bad boys to do that in some sort of secret club? She had to wonder. Maybe they even had a secret handshake. She'd have to ask him, if she ever got the nerve to. Finally she resorted to biting her lip until she almost drew blood to keep from laughing. Deep down she knew that if she took him seriously, it would spell trouble. Better that she keep herself distant. Not that a man like him would ever be interested in a woman like her. Tim had been attractive in a nice sort of way, but he hadn't been the kind of man that made a woman ache just when he looked at her. Men like that were rare and so dangerous to a woman's heart.

"Sorry, long days researching tend to make me a bit loopy. I take it you're ready to go into Weymouth?" She looked out the window, and to her astonishment, it was nearly sunset. Richard's story had consumed her.

"We will take your car. Do you have the keys?" He walked up to her and held out his hand expectantly.

"My car? Okay." She retrieved the car keys from her briefcase, careful to keep Richard's journal safely out of sight as she handed them over.

He took them, studied the key fob, and glowered. "A Honda?" His mouth pinched into a flat line.

"What's wrong with a Honda?" she demanded. The little

car had been great so far.

"Nothing." The way he said that one word betrayed how he really felt.

"Then why don't we take your car?"

He scoffed. "No. Not tonight. I try to keep a low profile when I go into town."

She gathered her things, returned the other books she'd been studying back to the shelves and jogged after him.

"A low profile?"

His face darkened as he looked down at her. "Yes. The locals aren't fond of me because of the damned curse they think I'm dragging around, and the tourists love me. Either way, I get too much attention. I try to stay here and only go into town if necessary."

Her heart splintered a little. He couldn't go into Weymouth without being persecuted all because of his family's string of bad luck? She couldn't imagine what that was like, but it had to be horrible.

"Is it like that in London?"

He shook his head and held the library door open for her. "No. In London I'm just another nobleman, famous and all that, but no one there cares about…the past."

She could almost hear the words left unspoken. He wanted to feel at home here in Weymouth, where his heart was and his family came from, not London. Yet a curse—or at least the rumors of one—was keeping him from being welcome even in his own home.

He led her through a maze of corridors in silence. She was fine with that, and he seemed to want to brood. When they reached the front door, Randolph was there to open it for them.

"I'll have dinner waiting for you when you return, my lord." The butler smiled warmly, and she smiled back. It was a comfort to see that someone genuinely cared about Bastian and his well-being. Why that mattered to her, she couldn't quite say; she only knew that it did.

"Thank you, Randolph; I won't be long."

As they approached the car, she headed for the right side, patting her pockets, only to remember she didn't have the keys. Bastian joined her by the door, keys in hand, and he waved for her to go around to the passenger side.

"Why?" She crossed her arms over her chest and stared at him.

He placed one hand on the roof of the car next to her shoulder and leaned into her, trapping her against the driver-side door. He gave her a scorching look while the corner of his mouth kicked up into a cocky grin.

"I *always* drive when a lady is involved. The cliffs are dangerous at night and the roads, too. I wouldn't want anything to happen to you while you're a guest here." He moved his other hand to her hip and brushed his fingers along her waist in a slow, intoxicating caress. Tingles of awareness flooded her entire body as the world seemed to shrink into that one featherlight touch. It was so easy to just let go when he touched her and not fight the passion that swelled inside her. But she had to stay in control.

She couldn't let him in. Not after Tim… Jane swallowed hard. The memories of other nights with another man she'd been so attracted to swamped her. Another man who hadn't believed her connection to Stormclyffe, her dreams of the past. Another man who thought she was crazy. The pain in her chest was strong enough that she closed her eyes, praying for the self-control to compose herself. Now was not the time to fall apart because her broken heart still stung. Bastian made it so easy for her to remember what it was like to be attracted to a man, to long for that close intimacy and the thrill of desire and longing.

Be flippant, keep him at a distance.

"I bet you do this all the time. Talk a woman out of driving with that smile."

He dropped his hand and shrugged in a casual way that showed just how comfortable he was in his own body. She envied that.

"Is it working?" He waggled his eyebrows, making her laugh. He kept her on her toes. One minute brooding, the next teasing. She didn't want to like him, but it was hard not to when he teased her.

"Maybe a little," she admitted. "I just prefer to drive, that's all."

"What is it with you Americans and driving? I've never met one who didn't think they should be behind the wheel," he said.

She tried not to laugh. "You may drive, my lord, if it will ease your need to repress a *colonial*." They were so close this time that when he smiled the effect of his nearness made her knees buckle.

"You're appeasing me, but I'll take my victory." He stepped back from her, chuckling and muttered "colonial" as she walked to the passenger side of the car.

When they got in, the first thing Bastian did after buckling his seat belt was flip the radio on. He started driving down the narrow road and hit the scan button, pausing when an oldie came on. He settled back, his lips curved in a small smile. She had to bite her lips to keep from singing along. It was one of her guilty pleasures. There was something innately freeing about letting go and just singing. This song was particularly hard to resist. It was one of her dad's favorites called "Don't Pull Your Love Out" by Hamilton, Joe Frank, & Reynolds. Unable to resist, she hummed as softly as possible.

"Go on, sing. I can tell you want to." He took his eyes off the road for a few seconds and glanced at her.

"Shut up."

He chuckled and cranked the volume dial up, and soon the car was filled with the song. She started when he began to sing. The Earl of Weymouth had a beautiful baritone. His British accent faded as he belted out the lyrics.

"Join me." He slipped in this command while the trumpets pelted out a quick melody in between versus.

"Fine." She surrendered.

She wasn't the most spectacular singer, but she wasn't cringe-worthy either. They matched pitches and crooned together as though they had sung a thousand times together over a thousand years. The feeling of déjà vu crept through her on cat's paws. She had never done this before, yet flashes of an unknown memory dug into her mind, sliding through years of memories she knew belonged to her. These slivers of conflicting images, hazy as morning mist, gave her a sudden headache. Putting her hands to her temples, she rubbed at the tender spots, hoping to ease the strange pain. It relented just a few seconds before Bastian looked her way. She answered his questioning gaze with a smile, hoping to hide her slight distress.

Ahead of them the sun had turned from peach to bloodred as it sank into the horizon. The nerves and jitters she'd had all day seemed to fade as he drove them toward town. When the song ended and another one began, he turned the volume back down to a soft background noise.

"I knew you would be fun," he declared.

"I knew you would be arrogant," she retorted, but there was no real bite in her tone. She enjoyed his teasing, now that she'd figured him out, or at least part of him. He kept his distance and tried to be off-putting to strangers to keep safe, just like her. But he slipped every now and then, letting her see a different man, someone carefree and happy. She hoped the man singing in the car was the real Bastian. The brooding, jaded man he presented himself as wasn't quite the same, like a shadow of his true self, a shadow distorted and fractured by years of loneliness and tragedy.

His past was full of pain and disappointment. He'd lost his father at a pivotal age in his life, and the responsibilities of his title and estate were a heavy burden he'd borne alone. The appearance of his easy life, with model girlfriends, fast cars, and parties, was probably an illusion he created to keep the bleak past and uncertain future at bay. Sometimes pretending to be something else, or masking who you truly were, was the safest thing to do.

She understood that. As a kid, she had known she wanted to study history and had taken school seriously. She had never tried to be something she wasn't, but sometimes she'd been tempted for just a moment here or there to change herself to escape the harsh judgments passed by her peers.

The rest of the drive into town was quiet but pleasant. Bastian seemed lost in his thoughts. He navigated the streets with ease, despite the flocks of tourists drifting in front of them like brightly colored birds.

"Where are you staying?"

"A little local inn two blocks from here."

He followed directions she gave him and pulled up in the first available parking space half a block away. Although the streetlights had turned on, the corner where they parked was still dark. He locked the car and pocketed the keys. A heavy silence settled between them, and he stared into the darkness, his face suddenly turned ashen. A woman stood just at the edge where the lamplight kissed shadows. It was impossible to see the woman's face, but the weight of her attention felt like twin holes boring into her skull. A primordial fear stabbed her chest and clouded her mind. She struggled to form words.

"Bastian, I know I've been enough trouble, but do you think you could walk me to the door?" She sounded pathetic, but she didn't feel safe walking to the inn alone. Something about that woman…

He didn't reply; instead he continued to watch the woman, his lips pursed into a frown. Did she unsettle him, too?

"You don't have to come with me." It cost everything she had to say that. The second she was able, she'd just run straight for the inn's door.

"You aren't staying here tonight. You'll get your things and check out immediately. I'll have Randolph prepare you dinner and a room."

"What?" Stay? At Stormclyffe with him? Her jaw slackened and she knew she must have looked ridiculous.

He shot her a quick, distracted look before returning his focus to the woman at the end of the street. "You'll stay with me. Don't try to argue. I won't hear otherwise."

Argue? Why would she argue against that? She tried not to show her relief as she glanced about the strangely empty street. Raucous sounds from the pub nearby seemed muted now that night fallen. A light breeze flowed across her face, and she rubbed her arms to warm up. He noticed and shrugged off his coat, holding it out. Before she could protest, he strode up to her.

"Jane, put the bloody coat on," he growled low, and she let him slide it up over her shoulders. The carefree man from their car ride was gone. The man looming over her was brooding and edgy. His gaze jumped from one building to the next as though expecting trouble.

"Let's get inside." He tucked her arm in his, the gesture less romantic and more of an attempt to get her to move. With a quick look over her shoulder, she exhaled. The woman half-wreathed in shadows had vanished.

When they got to the weathered wooden door of the inn, he slowly raised his head and stared at the creaking painted sign.

"The White Lady?" His voice was low and soft, as though

troubled.

"Er…yes. It's a very old historical place; that's what the website said anyway."

Bastian's focus fell on her, his expression reproachful. "Did you choose it because it was her family's?" His hands clenched into frightening fists at his sides. "Did you find it amusing to bring me here?"

She frowned and stepped back, suddenly afraid. Not of him, not exactly, but something crawled beneath her skin, and the hairs on the back of her neck rose. What was he talking about?

"What are you saying?"

"Isabelle Braxton. This inn belonged to her family." He whirled away, looking ready to storm off.

"What?" Suddenly she couldn't breathe. The flood of fear and the memories of her nightmares closed in, destroying her ability to suck in a breath. She collapsed against the Inn's wall and braced herself against it for support.

All this time, she'd planned her trip, come here, and spent one night, never knowing it was Isabelle's. Bastian had walked about fifteen feet away when he stopped, then slowly turned to face her. He crossed his arms and stared at her.

"You didn't know, did you?" He took a few steps toward her.

She wasn't paying attention to him, not fully. The image of the women in the white nightgown on the cliffs kept replaying in her mind. Her gaze drifted up to the sign. How had she been so stupid and missed the obvious connection between Isabelle and the inn?

"Jane?" He cupped her face in his hands and forced her to look at him.

His touch jolted her back to herself, banishing the memories.

"I didn't know… I didn't see the connection."

The hardness in his expression softened.

"I'm sorry. I thought you were poking fun at me," he admitted. "Let's go inside. The quicker we can get you checked out, the better."

She was grateful when he took her hand in his and led her to the inn's door. His palm was warm and strong. The touch was a comfort she hadn't expected him to offer. Which one was the real earl? The brooding, jaw-snapping wolf, or the playful, seductive man who sang in the car? Her thoughts were interrupted by the innkeeper coming to meet them at the door. He was in his early sixties, and a pair of thick glasses perched on his slightly bulbous nose.

"Miss Seyton. How are you?" he asked and then froze when he caught sight of Bastian.

"My lord," he hastily greeted. "I would have prepared the place if I had known you were coming."

Bastian waved a hand. "It is fine. I'm here to assist Miss Seyton. She is staying at the Hall, and we've come to collect her things and check her out. I will settle her bill and cover the remaining days she had planned on staying here."

When the innkeeper opened his mouth to argue, Bastian fixed him with a pointed look.

"You really don't need to—" Jane tried to say she would pay, but he shook his head at her in exasperation.

"Go on." He waved a hand imperiously.

With a frustrated little groan, she climbed the stairs to the second floor, Bastian trailing behind her. She pulled out the thick brass key and slid it into the door lock. He leaned against the wall only a foot away, waiting for her to open it. When she raised her head, she found his heated stare fixed upon her. For a second, neither of them moved, and the tension between them was an almost tangible force. Then the lock clicked, and she was jolted into awareness of herself again.

Once she was inside, she threw everything into her

LAUREN SMITH   63

suitcases as fast as she could. There would be time to organize it all later. When she emerged from the bathroom, she found Bastian standing by the window. The fading light of the sunset created a haunting silhouette. He could have passed for his ancestor with the striking profile he presented. Not that she had ever seen Richard, except for a faded color photograph of the only portrait Richard had ever commissioned of himself. But it had been enough. Bastian possessed many of the same features. One of his hands was pressed against the glass, fingers spread as though he was straining to reach through the window for something far beyond his reach. An echo of the wrenching sadness she had experienced when she glimpsed the woman in white came back to her. What was Bastian longing for?

"Hey." She broke the spell with that single word, and he looked over his shoulder at her. For a brief moment, his face was open, every emotion laid for her to see. The sheer vulnerability and fear-tinged melancholy ghosted behind his eyes, and it made her drift toward him. Then he twisted his lips into a cold, mocking smile—whether at himself or her, she wasn't sure.

"Finished packing?" He gestured to the toiletry bag she'd tossed on the bed.

"Oh, yes." She snatched the bag, tucked it into her suitcase, and zipped it up. She was eager to leave the inn now that she knew its dark and sad history. It felt too personal to be here. Funny, she felt more comfortable at Stormclyffe.

"Then let's be gone. Randolph will have dinner ready soon."

He bent to grab her suitcase at the same time she reached for it. Their heads collided in a painful crack.

"Ouch!" She stumbled, and the back of her knees collided with the bed behind. She fell onto the soft, quilted comforter, and as Bastian tried to catch her, he tripped over the rolling suitcase and collapsed right on top of her. The air whooshed out of her lungs, and she sucked in a desperate gasp of air. Their bodies pressed together perfectly, her breasts against his chest, their noses close enough to brush. His eyes were warm and dark and her insides twisted a little as desire awakened within her.

Ever since Tim had left her six months ago, she'd felt closed off. Yet, as their bodies melded on the bed by sheer accident, it felt right. Her hands cupped his shoulders, and his muscles tensed beneath her fingers. He wasn't built like a body builder, but he had that perfect lithe figure that was all strength and lean lines of perfect muscle. What would he look like with his clothes off? She cursed herself for wanting to know.

"My apologies." His groan escaped through gritted teeth, and he rolled off her and onto his back beside her.

"It's okay," she said. "I'm sorry we knocked heads."

He chuckled, even though it sounded pained. "It would be more fun to…what do you Americans call it…knock boots?"

She put a hand to her chest and breathed out. "Just when I think you might actually be one of those English gentlemen I keep hearing about…"

She left the rest unsaid, as he sniggered like a misbehaving schoolboy.

"I'm not a gentleman. I'm cursed. At least according to the townspeople." His tone changed, his anger thickening the words, as though his curse was something he'd brought about, not something thrust upon him by his ancestors. It frightened her, not that she thought he would hurt her, but she wondered whether he might be right. Her notes from earlier today hadn't lied. Women who married into the Stormclyffe line died early and painfully. He had every reason to push her away, and she didn't want to be in the path of a curse. There was no sense in taking a chance and putting herself at risk.

"I'm sorry I tripped you." She glanced away, trying to ignore her body's reaction to him. Even though he no longer touched her, the phantom pressure of his body seemed to linger. Her skin heated, and her heart beat fast at the mere memory of his body on top of hers. Like the encounter in the drawing room, she wanted to be wild, untamed, to have that gorgeous aristocratic mouth of his seeking sensitive places on her skin until she screamed for him to take her. Unlike the passionate clinch in the drawing room that led to her shameless orgasm at the magic of his hands, this felt real and concrete, not like ancient phantoms had taken hold of her body.

When he rose and picked up her suitcase, she followed with a weary sigh. Her forehead hurt like hell. She'd probably have a nasty knot later. There was no sign of the innkeeper as they came back down the stairs and paused at the front desk. Bastian braced his forearms on the counter and leaned over to peer into the small workroom behind the check-in area. There was no sign of obvious life from the small room. With a sigh, he turned his attention to the small brass bell and smacked it with his palm. The loud *ding* was jarring in the silence. Still, no movement, no sound, not a whisper of life emanated from anywhere inside the old inn.

"Is there anyone else staying here? Any other guests?"

"Um…" She racked her mind, trying to recall if she'd actually seen anyone.

She hadn't.

He seemed to understand her silence, and his lips pursed. "Very well."

It was a very British thing to do, and she almost laughed. Smiling and laughing always came naturally when she was anxious, afraid, or upset. It was a horrible personality trait, one she despised about herself, but she couldn't help it. It had certainly made for some awkward situations in the past, and this was no different. When he raised that one brow, she knew he had picked up on her inappropriate reaction.

He retrieved a white card from his wallet and hastily scrawled a message on it, putting it on the counter.

"Hopefully, the innkeeper will find this and contact me about the bill." He slipped his wallet back into his pocket.

"You really don't need do that," she said.

He didn't reply but grabbed her bag and headed for the door. When they stepped outside, it seemed that the darkness practically swallowed them up. It consumed the streets, and even the lights from the pub next door barely penetrated the gloom. She snuggled deeper into Bastian's coat, inhaling the masculine scent of him. She should give it back. His scent was too good, and she hated that she liked it. A distant streetlight a block away was the only beacon they had to guide them back to her rental car.

With a burst of laughter and chatter, a gaggle of young women suddenly stumbled out of the pub. Bastian and Jane both spun at the unexpected sound. Even as drunk as the woman appeared to be, they were able to recognize Bastian.

"Oh my God! It's him! The hot duke with the haunted mansion or whatever."

Jane could have slapped the girl. The women were American and sadly stupid. She silently prayed that Bastian wouldn't hold their idiocy against her. It wasn't even worth correcting them. The women suddenly flocked around them, like angry geese, squawking as they tried to get close to him.

"Excuse me, ladies." His words were a low, rumbling murmur that seemed to only heighten their fervor and excitement.

A red haze descended over Jane's vision as one of the women dragged a red-nailed hand down Bastian's chest. He danced back a step like a boxer dodging a blow, only to find he was surrounded. When he met Jane's gaze, he silently begged for her mercy. There was only one way to deal with these women. She put two fingers between her lips and whistled. The shrill sound cut through the women squabbling over him, and he used the distraction to shove his way clear of them.

"Hey!" one of the women snapped when she realized her prey was escaping. "Come back!"

Jane trotted to catch up with Bastian, but they couldn't shake the group of women. They had only progressed twenty feet from the inn door when a shout halted them in their tracks. Jane bumped into Bastian's back with an oomph! His free hand instantly caught her around the shoulders steadying her.

"You hitting on my girlfriend, asshole?" An American man suddenly appeared in front of Bastian and Jane in the direction they'd been trying to flee.

How in the hell? Jane wondered where the man had come from. It obviously hadn't been the inn. He held a cigarette in one hand. The tip burned orange in the night as he sucked on it, then flicked it down at Bastian's feet. Her lips parted, a thousand angry words ready to spew forth, but Bastian still had his arm around her shoulder, and his fingers dug into the coat slightly, as though encouraging her to remain silent. The man in front of them continued to wait for a moment to see if they would answer.

She tried to make out his features, but it was too dark to see more than a rather unremarkable face, possibly bordering on unattractive. Bastian was an inch or two taller than him but wasn't nearly as muscled. This guy could have been a professional weightlifter. He probably popped steroids like candy. She tried to breathe and not panic.

Five more muscled men emerged from the dark behind the first man.

"Answer me!" The man's shout reverberated off the brick walls the concrete pavement.

"Let us pass. We have no interest in your lady or her

friends." Bastian's voice carried the authority of his noble heritage, but it was completely lost on the muscled idiot in front of them.

"This guy hit on you, right, Candi?"

One of the women, the one who'd been stroking Bastian's chest a few seconds before, stepped out of the crowd, wearing a tight miniskirt and a pink tank top. Jane hated when her fellow Americans became stereotypical bad tourists.

"He did. He sure did. He even kissed me." Candi's red lips twisted into a wicked smile, one that Jane wanted to smack right off her face.

"He did not kiss you. We don't even know you!" Jane fired back. This entire situation was insane. They were being accosted by strangers, and there wasn't a sign of any police. Shouldn't they be patrolling Weymouth after dark?

Bastian's lips pursed into a thin line and exasperation narrowed his eyes as he spoke to the men blocking their way. "Please let us pass. We are tired, and it is late. We have no quarrel with you."

"Who the hell do you think you are, huh? Kissing my girl? You're gonna pay!" The man dove for Bastian.

In one swift move, Bastian shoved Jane away from him and out of the line of danger and had only seconds to dodge the swinging fist. He managed it, barely.

"Get him!" The man ordered his friends to join in the fray. The women all staggered back drunkenly on their high heels trying to avoid getting in the middle of what Jane feared was going to be a huge fight. One with terrible odds.

The thugs surged toward Bastian, and suddenly fists were flying in the dark. It was a dance of living shadows as the men battled each other, accompanied by a symphony of sickening bones crunching and agonized grunts.

"Bastian!" Jane screamed. Terror spiked through her, raking her insides with claws. God, those men could kill him!

He answered with a roar of sheer rage and suddenly one of the men careened past her as though shoved by someone in the melee, and he collided with the brick wall of the inn. His head hit first, and the unpleasant sound of skull smashing against stone indicated he was out of the fight for good. His body slumped down to the ground. His eyelids fluttered, and he huffed out a breath. Thank God the man was alive. The women who had been watching the fight eagerly started to back away at the sight of the unconscious man.

"Get out of here!" Jane shouted at them and stepped toward them menacingly. She pulled out her cell phone. "I'm calling the police!" She dialed the number but didn't hit send. The last thing Bastian needed was police swarming him if they could help it. It would only further blacken his name, and he'd probably end up in the local papers. If she could get the women to leave, it might break up the fight.

The woman, Candi, didn't move, even as her friends scattered like mice. A cold malevolence gleamed in her eyes as she put her hands on her hips and glared at Jane.

"He's mine. He'll *always* be mine." The tone of her voice changed from silky to raspy, as though two different voices struggled for control of her throat.

"What?" Her skin crawled as she stared at the other woman. It reminded her of how she'd felt a short while earlier when the woman at the end of the street had been looking at her. It made her feel as though hundreds of spiders scuttled along her flesh and crawled into the pit of her stomach.

Candi blinked, and the look of seething hatred was gone, replaced by inebriated confusion. She turned and ran back into the pub. The second she was gone, Jane focused on the fight again. Three men were still throwing punches with a vengeance, but Bastian was holding up okay so far. He wouldn't be able to stay on top of the fight much longer. Jane dove into the fray.

Chapter Five

Pain exploded in Bastian's skull as one of the men backhanded him. It would only take a few more strikes like these, and he'd go down. He had been worried a confrontation like this would happen, but he'd gone on this fool's errand simply to spend more time with Jane.

One of the men lunged for him as two more circled, waiting like wolves. Bastian slid sideways to avoid the man that dove for them, his feet skidding along the concrete. The move cost him greatly as he stumbled and fell. Instinct had him rolling back up onto the balls of his feet in a squat position, but he was vulnerable. A booted foot dug into his ribs in a savage kick, and his lungs expelled every breath of air in him. Fractures of pain shot through his chest. It took every ounce of willpower to gather his strength and tackle the man who had kicked him by grabbing the man's legs and dragging him to the ground.

Jane's frightened cry sent his senses scattering as fear for what was happening to her took over. Suddenly she was flying over his crouched body, tripping over him really, as she tried to escape the grasp of another of the men. She recovered from her fall and scrambled backward. The man pursuing her wasn't so lucky. When he collided with Bastian, Bastian pivoted to the side and grabbed the man's grubby plaid shirt, using the man's momentum to propel him forward and down. He flew face first into the pavement, and then he didn't move. In the dim lights from the pub, Bastian could just make out the dark smear of blood near his head. The fallen man moaned but didn't get up.

"Jane?" Bastian called out as he struggled to get up, scraping his palms over the cold concrete.

The man Bastian had tackled earlier still had fight left in him and managed one last punch to Bastian's eye before Bastian laid him flat with knockout blow to his temple. A feminine groan ahead of him was his only hint as to where she'd landed. He found her next to her suitcase, bending over it as she studied its ruined state. He could barely make out the scene, but he saw that her groan was one of frustration and anger. The canvas suitcase was lying in a pool of water where faint streetlights glinted off the shallow pool. No doubt her clothes and any other items inside were soaked. It was his fault they'd been attacked. He couldn't set foot in town without attracting trouble and attention, whether he tried to avoid it or not. This was exactly why he shouldn't have come with her tonight, but he couldn't trust her to drive alone, not after his father had died trying to make the drive back to the Hall.

"Damn." She righted the suitcase and rolled it over to where he stood on the curb, watching her. He was closer to the lights from the pub than she was, and when she caught sight of him, she gasped and ran straight up to him.

"Oh my God! Are you okay?" She grasped his face, and he flinched as several sensitive places on his cheeks and jaw protested, despite the gentleness of her touch.

"I've been better. This is exactly why I insisted you stay at Stormclyffe." He pushed her hands away and touched the back of his head, wincing because it felt like glass shards were embedded in the back of his skull. There wasn't a wound, only a nasty bump. Jane's hands returned to his face. They were soft and soothing as she examined him. The unexpected touch pulled something deep inside him. He wanted her to keep touching him, but he couldn't let her. She was already too close to him, and his family's bad luck was starting to extend to her.

"You're a mess. Come on, we need to get you fixed up." She looped one arm through his and led him back to the car, dragging her suitcase behind her with her free hand. The growing pain of the new headache set in, and Bastian handed over the keys to the rental car without much of a fight. Driving the way he felt now wasn't safe or wise.

She drove them to a nearby pharmacy that was open late and ran in to buy supplies. While she was gone, Bastian pulled out his phone and dialed Randolph.

"Yes, my lord?" His butler answered on the first ring.

"We will be a little late. Please have the cook prepare some sandwiches and leave them in the kitchen."

"Of course, my lord. Do you require anything else?"

He smiled, even though it hurt to do so. Randolph was a good man. He was one of Bastian's father's servants who had remained loyal over the years and had known Bastian since he was a babe in his cradle. Too often of late, the butler had been carrying the burden of the renovations, and the man deserved a reprieve.

"No, nothing else. Thank you, Randolph. Get to bed and rest."

For a long moment, the older man didn't respond, but when he did speak, his tone was a little rough and full of appreciation. "Thank you, my lord. I shall see you in the morning."

"Good night." He ended the call and pocketed his phone just in time to catch Jane's quick-footed approach from the store, a plastic bag slung over one arm. His lips twitched. She was playful and casual, her American upbringing warring with her love for British culture. She was a conundrum that fascinated him. The way she moved, with a dancer's grace, every action natural and real, not like the women of his station who carried themselves with rigid poise or the women he dated who hung all over him, batting their lashes coquettishly. Jane simply existed as she was, and he liked that in a woman. He liked it too much.

I cannot get attached. The grim reminder didn't sit well with him. She needed to finish her research and get out. He hoped she wouldn't find much to write about. The last thing he wanted was a research paper pointing like a sign to his home so that all the tourists coming to the castle would end up being ghost hunters or simply curious gawkers.

She opened the door with one hand and tossed the bag into his lap. When she saw his face, she wrinkled her nose and squinted.

"Does it look that bad?" he asked.

She bit her lip then replied. "I should have grabbed a bag of frozen peas."

Peas? What on earth did the woman need peas for? When a man got into a fight and had bruising, he didn't put a bag of bloody peas on his face. A bag of ice would have been better.

"When you get out onto the country road, go slow, Jane." He wished he could drive. He didn't like the idea of her steering them to their doom.

"Okay. Why?" She wasn't questioning him or challenging him. He didn't hear that in her tone.

"The road is very narrow, and there are cliffs and plenty of ditches within easy distance of the road where you could roll the car. I was not joking when I said earlier you could easily harm yourself or worse." He braced one hand on the right armrest and the other against the closed window as the pain in his head doubled. The memories were always buried deep in his heart, but having to drive the road that had killed his father wasn't something he faced easily.

"Are you sure you're okay? You're really pale." Something in his chest gave a funny little flip at the look of concern she gave him. No one except for Randolph or his parents had ever worried about him the way she seemed to. His little bookworm cared.

"It feels like an ax is splitting my head in two." He rubbed his temples again.

"There's aspirin and a bottle of water in the sack." She pointed to the bag in his lap.

With a sigh, he dug through it until he found the bottle and the water, and he downed two pills. Hopefully the medicine would kick in soon and dull the awful throbbing between his eyes.

"Bastian...I'm so sorry about what happened."

He shrugged and set the water in the cup holder. "It wasn't your fault some drunken louts decided to have some fun."

The look she cast his way was doubtful. "Is this the sort of thing that happens when you come into Weymouth?"

He nodded. This had certainly been one of the more violent encounters but no less disturbing than the other incidents he'd had. The last time he had been in town, an old Russian woman outside a butcher shop had spat at his feet and made a strange sign with her hands, which he later learned was a sign to ward off the devil or evil spirits. Sometimes he wondered if he was a magnet for bad attention because of his family's reputation or the "curse" as the townspeople viewed it. Less reputable characters often flocked to him, ready to wreak havoc upon his life.

"These things happen. I took a chance going there."

"Why did you?" she asked.

Her eyes were on the road, but he knew her attention was fixated on him and what he might say. The truth couldn't hurt.

"I wanted to. It was that simple." If she'd gone alone, she might have been fine, but then again, he couldn't be sure, which is why he'd risked going with her. Only that had brought down the trouble all the more quickly upon them both.

She glanced at him. "I don't think there's anything simple about you."

Neither of them spoke after that. The car headlights pierced the gloom ahead of them, revealing the pale gray pavement of the road. Without the moon to light the hills, the terrain was pitch-black. Even the lights from the city behind them seemed to be cocooned in a bubble, unable to penetrate the darkness of the sloping hills that led to his family's home.

A flash of memory crossed his mind of the first night he'd come to the hall. It had been an endless night like this. A childlike fear of the dark and the things that stirred in it had risen up in him so quickly, he'd sucked in a harsh breath. In that instant, he'd longed for his father more than anything else. He envied the way his father had never seemed to fear anything. Driving to the Hall near midnight would have been the same to his father as driving there during daylight. It wasn't like that for Bastian. He was a sensible man, a rational one, but sometimes his body reacted, even when his head insisted there was nothing to fear from foolish stories and old wives' tales.

As he'd driven up to Stormclyffe Hall that first night before starting the renovations, the monolithic specter of the castle had burst out of the gloom, appearing before his headlights like a phantom itself. Not a single light had shone from the windows, nor had a breath of life stirred in the air around him as he got out of the car. He'd wondered then, would restorations and updated plumbing scrub the stones of the blood of his ancestors, purge the thought of curses and ghosts from the minds of nearly all of England—and one American PhD student? He hadn't been able to answer the question but only rely on the hope that all would be well if he could but restore the castle.

He was so lost in these dark thoughts, he failed to notice they had arrived at the Hall.

"Let's get inside and see to those injuries." Jane was already out of the car and fetching her suitcase. Bastian grabbed the pharmacy bag and joined her at the entrance. He unlocked the door, and once they were inside, took her suitcase and rolled it to the kitchens. The original kitchens of the hall had been a large stone-floored room. The remodeling had added advanced cooktops, several ovens, three fridges, and a dazzling array of lighting fixtures that made the new appliances gleam.

"I called Randolph while you were inside the shop. There should be sandwiches left out for us."

She nodded and started getting out the supplies. "Sit." She pointed at a bar stool that backed up to one of the side counters. He did as she commanded, curious to see what she would do next. With an air of an army general, she prepped a makeshift nurse's station. Dipping the edge of one cloth into hydrogen peroxide, she then dabbed at the cut on his face. He bit the inside of his cheek as the treatment burned. She handled several more small scrapes on his arm and hands before finally slapping a few Band-Aids on the deeper cuts. Her touch was gentle, her fingers soothing as they drifted over his skin.

"It's my turn to play doctor." He couldn't resist the chance to tease her, even though he knew he shouldn't. Teasing could lead to so much more. Things he couldn't do, not when he needed to stay the bloody hell away from her before some ridiculous coincidence "proved" the curse to yet another person—particularly one who might just get her assertions published. But damn if he couldn't resist.

The responding blush that flooded her cheeks was priceless. She started to pull her hands away, but he caught her wrists and held her close. Her lips were ripe for kissing and oh so close.

Christ...he wanted her so bad it hurt and not in a way related to the injuries of his fight. The need to have her was as strong as the need to draw his next breath. It was nothing like before, when they first met. This time there was no wild, frightening fire driving him to act in a state of madness. Instead, there was a deep ache only curable by her touch, her body tucked in his arms. He wanted to explore her, learn what made her sigh and purr. The incident in the drawing room had been a flash fire of passion quick to burn out. Right now though, it was vastly different. His attraction to her wasn't a fleeting thing that would vanish when sanity returned.

Temporary lust was easily managed. True desire was an entirely different thing.

Still holding her hand, he noticed a few scrapes on her knuckles and some faint bruising marring her creamy skin.

"How many punches did you throw?" He meant to tease her, but his words come out rough. The idea of her fighting made his blood heat and yet made him anxious, too. She was under his protection, and she'd gotten hurt. Guilt rotted away inside him.

"I might have thrown a few." She faced him, her voice steady.

"Brave little bookworm," he mused.

Her eyes widened, and those luscious lips parted on a shocked gasp. "Bookworm?"

He swallowed, realizing he had let it slip. Time to distract her. He scooped up a clean cloth and dabbed at her knuckles.

"Ow!" she yelped. He could tell by the half-hidden smile on her lips that it hadn't really stung.

Bastian continued to clean the scrapes before fixing a few plasters around her fingers. The entire time she watched him, and he feared she could see right through him. No woman had ever looked upon him with such startling clarity. Her gaze unmade him and reformed him into something he'd longed to be for years: unguarded, open, and unafraid. She was the sort of woman that could tempt him to risk everything to be with her, if only he let himself. And that was exactly the problem. He couldn't let her get close, not when what was left of his family and their reputation might get hurt.

When he was finished tending to her, he gestured to one of the fridges.

"You get the food. I'll fetch something from the wine cellar."

"Sure." She tugged her hands from his and stepped back.

The loss of her closeness unsettled him, but he had no valid reason to drag her into his arms. He almost wished he'd lose himself like he had in the drawing room. Distance, even temporary, would be good. He didn't look back as he left the kitchen. The castle halls were dark. Half of the lighting in the halls still hadn't been installed yet. Luckily, the route to the wine cellar wasn't that complicated. A left turn past the painting of two knights jousting, then a right at the hall where Richard's collection of marble statues stood on pedestals on either side of the long room. It was one of the more intriguing parts of the house. He made mental note to keep her away from the private archives where the journals containing sordid details of the Weymouth tragedies lay.

The old oak door leading to wine cellar groaned as he pulled on the circular iron handle. The hinges needed oiling or perhaps replacing. One more thing to add to the damned list of things to fix. An electric lamp at the top of the stairs was within each reach, and he flicked it on. Yellow light bathed the steps but didn't penetrate the pool of blackness below. When Bastian took the first step down, a cool breeze tickled his face, stirring the fine hairs on the back of his neck. He didn't move as the sound of soft exhalation brushed his ears, like a woman's heavy sigh. He could almost hear Jane's voice in his head.

Ghosts, they haunt these walls. She had never uttered the words aloud, but he had seen that thought flash across her face.

When his feet hit the stone floor at the bottom of the stairs, he paused again. The curious sensation of focus on the back of his head made him uneasy. It had to be nerves. Jane and her foolish obsession were rubbing off on him, that was all. However…he didn't linger in the cellar. He snatched up the nearest bottle of red wine from the rack to his right and vaulted back up the stairs, firmly slamming the cellar door behind him with a satisfying *bang*. Whatever was down there, if there was anything, would stay down there. As he headed back for the kitchen, he strained to focus on a faint sound… the echoing laugh of a woman.

Chapter Six

Jane studied the plate of cucumber sandwiches, a little smile tugging at her lips. Cucumber sandwiches. Wasn't that so English? Her stomach rumbled, and she succumbed to her hunger and reached for one of the perfectly cut little pieces.

"Gotcha." Bastian chuckled from somewhere behind her.

She whirled around, a sandwich stuffed in her mouth and guilt heating her cheeks. After swallowing she apologized.

"Sorry, I'm starved." She half turned and picked up the plate, offering him one.

He selected two and set them on a small plate for himself. Then he crossed the room to the cabinets on the far wall and retrieved two wineglasses, filling them.

There was something so intimate about the two of them alone in the kitchen, ready to share a meal. It wasn't at all what she had expected when she came here. It was one of the things she and Tim had often done. Meals, just the two of them in cozy little pubs in Charleston on the holidays. It made her heart ache and twist because she missed the man less than the intimacy of just being with someone. She had to be careful.

She didn't want that intimacy ever again, even as much as she missed it. The thought of losing someone she loved over all the strange happenings in her life tied to Stormclyffe hurt too much.

She shivered, realizing she still wore his coat. She would return it, soon, but not right now. Surely there was nothing wrong with wanting to savor a few more minutes of being enveloped by a coat that bore his woodsy, masculine scent. It was soothing and enticing, like her own personal catnip.

"So, tell me about yourself, Jane. I realized today I know very little of you except for your academic interests, of course." He slid her glass close to her hand. Their fingers met on the glass's stem, and neither of them pulled away for a moment. It was Jane who finally broke the contact, and she wished she hadn't, but she desperately needed a drink. She wasn't great at small talk. With Tim, everything had been so easy; they'd had so much in common. But Bastian was a stranger, one she felt drawn to in ways she never had felt with Tim. What could she say?

I'm just a girl who had an average, happy life but always felt I belonged somewhere else...belonged...here? It sounded silly, and if she was going to start talking about herself, she needed a few sips of liquid courage. The wine's bouquet was heady and rich. She thought she tasted a hint of cherry and oak.

"Not much to tell really. I'm from Charleston, South Carolina."

"Siblings?" he prompted and then took a bite out of his sandwich.

"One brother. Garrett is four years older than me. He can be an idiot at times, but a loveable one." A little smile curved her lips.

He grinned devilishly. "That explains your instinct to punch my shoulder whenever you're losing an argument."

"Oh?" She tried not to laugh, but she couldn't help herself. It was true. She punched Garrett. A lot. He was always bullying her whenever they argued about something, and socking him was the best way to distract him. It was a habit she'd never really outgrown.

"A close friend of mine has a younger brother and sister, and you remind me of them." The soft smile that played on his lips melted her inside. He seemed genuinely happy at some secret memory from long ago. What she wouldn't give in that moment to discover a way to keep him smiling like that. It was a beautiful expression on his face, and someone blessed with that nice of a smile should have a reason to always be smiling. Yet, she knew only too well after this afternoon's research that smiles from Bastian were few and far between and hard-won if they came. There was so little for him to be happy about. It was obvious that wealth and title did not equal happiness. It was one more reason she was curious to know who would bring such fond memories and soft smiles to his lips.

"Who is it?" she couldn't help but ask. She desperately wanted some insight into his life and his past.

"Rhys Wolfe. You have probably heard of him by his title. Viscount Wolfe. He's a fellow schoolmate of mine from Eaton and later Cambridge. He's a good man. His younger brother Owen and his sister Chloe are quite the pair of troublemakers, always have been. They perfected the art of outnumbering and outmaneuvering Rhys at every opportunity, much to the hilarity of us watching whatever scheme they had concocted unfold. Afterward, they would insist it was Rhys's determination to be the perfect elder brother that inspired such a need to rebel and cause trouble. I sometimes wish—" He caught himself and with a rueful shake of his head, covered his lips with his wineglass, and drank.

She swallowed hard as she resisted the desire to ask the question that would prompt his answer. Perhaps if she changed tactics, she could get him to come back to it.

"What's it like? Growing up and living in this world?" She gestured to the kitchens.

"Being an earl, you mean?" He laughed softly, but there was no joy in the sound. Only pain.

"Try to imagine a dozen responsibilities, duties, and worries and multiply that by a thousand, extend it to a lifetime, and you'll have some idea of what being an earl is like. I spend most of my time worrying over issues in Parliament and my estate. I have to worry not only about my own needs but those of whom I employ." He raked his hands through his hair and then planted his elbows on the counter and continued in exasperation. "It's like running a bloody miniature country. Frustrating as hell," he growled. "The only time I ever was able to focus on something outside of my duties to my lands and title was when I was away at university."

Comprehension flooded Jane, and visions of the websites and news articles she'd read about him flashed across her eyes. A piece of the puzzle of Bastian Carlisle fell into place at last.

"That's why you pursued such extensive studies. I wondered at the number of degrees and the depth and complexity of your education." She slapped her hands over her mouth when she realized her words sounded like an insult.

His lips kicked up in a wolfish grin as she blushed to the roots of her hair.

"I mean to say…that is…most people in your position wouldn't waste time…" That didn't come out right either. She felt like an idiot.

He reached out and brushed an errant lock of her hair behind her ear, still grinning that devil's grin. "I know what you meant."

His touch made her skin tingle and her body flush, as his fingertips coasted over the sensitive shell of her ear.

They were so close on their bar stools. If she moved an

inch, their knees would touch.

"Learning was my only solace, my only freedom." He bit his bottom lip, appearing equally thoughtful and bashful, which turned out to have the most devastating effect on her body. Little shivers and heat flared and fired beneath her skin like sparklers on the fourth of July. She moved without thinking and reached for his bare forearm. His muscles jumped at her touch but he didn't draw back.

I shouldn't touch him. She knew it. Her head knew it, but her heart, still bruised and bleeding wanted so badly to connect to him, even if it meant risking itself for more hurt.

"It sounds very silly when I say it out loud," he mused and shook his head. The action was so disheartening that Jane acted on pure instinct.

She caught his face in her hands and pulled his head down to hers, kissing him. For a long second, only her lips moved, enticing his to respond, and then it was as if she'd unleashed a wild creature. Bastian caught her by the waist with one hand and by the nape of her neck with the other as he dragged her off her stool and onto his lap, forcing her to straddle him. The stumbling action of their coming together had him laughing against her neck as he steadied her. Then he took possession of her mouth again.

She was alone inside her head; no phantoms chased her and pushed her away from her own body. This wasn't like the drawing room. There was only this wild, raw kiss that felt as old as the stones on the cliff and as unceasing as the waves battering the rocks. Each nibble, each lingering lick and feathering of lips was alluring and dangerous. The need to be with him, to get closer even when their bodies touched everywhere, wasn't enough. And it was only a kiss. When had time shattered and the universe shrunk to just two bodies pressed together, two mouths fused as one? Never in her life had Jane experienced such a moment. It terrified her. Being with Tim hadn't felt like this, not even close. But like Tim, the earl thought she was nuts. *I need to stop. I need to break away from him before I lose myself.*

But it was too late; she was lost. His kiss would haunt her more than any spectral woman in white or leaping shadows. Her feelings, the ones she had refused to accept existed, were now forced into the light and could never be buried again.

As their lips parted reluctantly, he brushed her hair back from her face, his fingertips lingering on her skin and threading through her hair. That tender, intimate gesture squeezed her heart like a fist. Feeling this way, it was like a knife slicing small cuts on her soul. The pain wasn't there right away; it grew slowly as some rationality returned. This wasn't real. Whatever was between them was merely chemical attraction. He might have done this with many women before her—play the wounded Byronic hero and they'd all fall into his embrace. The realization left a bitter taste in her mouth and an ache in her chest.

Still, his passion-darkened eyes and ragged breathing were a sensual symphony. Their foreheads touched, and his hands massaged her shoulders in slow, methodical, soothing strokes. He nuzzled her, his face brushing against hers as he shut his eyes and exhaled. Jane gazed in rapt fascination at his incredibly long lashes, a deep gold like his hair, as they fanned out over his proud cheekbones. He was so beautiful it hurt her to look at him, yet she couldn't tear her eyes away.

"We should finish dinner." His hands dropped from her body. She nearly cried out from the loss of his touch. She finally sank back onto her bar stool, unsure of what to do. He did not meet her eyes, and they finished dinner quickly in silence. Did he regret what they'd done? Had he not liked kissing her? Her insecurities were fresh and unwelcome, but she couldn't push them away.

One thought ran through her mind again and again like

quicksilver.

I am falling for him, and he doesn't even care.

After dinner, she and Bastian took care of the dishes, and then he escorted her back into the corridor. Her suitcase was once again under his control, and Jane bit her lip to keep from frowning. Didn't he want to talk about what happened? Or was he going to just ignore the fact that they'd made out like a couple of teenagers? She wanted to talk about it. Hell, she wanted to prod him a bit and see how he felt about her. But the silence seemed pretty damning evidence. A man wouldn't just kiss a woman and then ignore her if he was really attracted to her. Which meant he didn't really desire her.

"Bastian, would it be possible to see more of the castle tomorrow?"

He studied one of the many paintings on the wall before answering. "I suppose Randolph could give you a tour of the house and grounds before you settle down with your books." He led her to one of the main staircases in the castle.

"Randolph? Not you?" Rejected. It didn't just sting. It hurt. Bad.

"It's better if we don't…" His words lingered like shadows, swallowing what little feeble light of hope her foolish heart had held. He cleared his throat. "Randolph is much more familiar with the recent history of the Hall and would be an excellent guide."

"But—"

"I have a lot to do. Your presence is already an imposition. I cannot waste time on you." Bastian didn't meet her eyes when he spoke. It might have killed her outright if he had.

Waste time on me? The idea that she was a waste was so belittling that it chilled her heart. She couldn't fall for a man who viewed her like that. She was worth time. If he didn't see that, then it was his loss. Whatever temporary insanity that had gripped her since she met him was obviously hormone related. Strictly physical. That was all it had to be.

"Your room is this way." He rested a palm on the dark oak banister. The wood gleamed beneath the glow of the wall sconce lights on either side of the stairs. Intricate flowers had been carved into the wood painting a picturesque view nearly tricking her into thinking they might be real, as if they had been painted. The petals and stems looked real enough that she could touch them and expect them to feel their softness. Bastian tapped, waiting to hear her answer. He seemed completely unaware of the beautiful banister next to him.

"This way." He started up the carpeted stairs. She followed behind him, hating how she couldn't help but admire the way his jeans molded to his backside. Memories from the drawing room filled her, how she'd wrapped her legs around his waist as he… She shivered and tried to push that thought away. That moment with him had been so different from the others. They'd come together as though they'd spent centuries apart, not as though they were newly discovering each other. She preferred the man who had kissed her in the kitchen, the man who sweetly kissed her with fire and passion but not with wild desperation and anger. That had felt like someone else. But of course, he didn't want her. Wasn't interested. She was a "waste of time." The thought made her bristle. Even though she didn't want to like him, she didn't want him to *not* like her.

When they reached her room, he opened the door, revealing a beautiful room done in the Baroque period style. The walls were a fashionable drab green, and a four-poster bed with crimson moreen hangings trimmed with forest-green tassels made an impressive sight. The crème coverlet was brocaded with flowers, and the bed looked plush and comfortable. A healthy fire snapped and crackled in the fireplace opposite the bed. It was the painting that hung above the bed that caught her attention.

"Oh!" Her hand flew to her throat, clasping her pendant

as she struggled to breathe. Excitement stirred to life inside her all over again as she stared up in wonder. Bastian set her luggage down next to her and joined her at the foot of the bed.

"It's him!" She pointed, even though the gesture was unnecessary.

"I thought you would enjoy this room."

Enjoy? There wasn't a word in the English language that could have described how she was feeling in that moment. She was staring at the only portrait of Richard Carlisle in existence. The one she had seen in her research books. The faded photographs didn't do it justice. Richard was seated in a red wingback chair facing her. An Irish wolfhound sat next to him, its tongue lolling to the side of its mouth like a dark guardian with a lupine smile. Richard's face mirrored his hound's but only with a hint of a smile. He was predatory, sensual, and powerful in his dark blue waistcoat, and knee-high black boots. Bastian's ancestor looked every inch the earl he was. But it was so much more than that. Bastian and Richard could have been twins, the uncanny resemblance was so strong.

The painting cast a spell over her, weaving invisible tendrils around her body, drawing her in. Barely audible whispers drifted close to her ears.

"My beloved, my beloved, you cannot run from me again."

"Cannot run," she murmured in a daze. A faint ringing started up in her ears, and she swayed uneasily on her feet. Bastian caught her by the elbow, steadying her. As soon as he touched her, it was gone.

"Are you all right?" Bastian asked.

"Just tired." She pulled away from him.

"I trust you will be comfortable here?" His gaze danced across the room as though trying to study it with a critical eye, looking for any faults.

Her own focus went straight back to the painting. "Yes!" she exclaimed, tearing her gaze from Richard to the living man next to her. "Thank you so much for letting me stay here." Despite his callous words, the gesture of letting her stay in this room wasn't lost on her. He could have just as easily put her in a broom cupboard, but instead he'd brought her here.

"You're welcome. Randolph is always around if you need anything. My room is across the hall. Breakfast is at eight, and I will inform Randolph he is to take you on the tour." He moved toward the door but paused, turned around to lean against the jamb, and look at her. His figure was shadowy as though caught between two worlds and belonging fully to neither. A strange stirring of woe and fear dug deep into her stomach. Jane had a horrible sense that she might lose him. With great sadness, she admitted in her heart that she knew he would never belong to her. No matter what dreams and hopes she might build, they were as solid as castles formed in the clouds. One could never possess what one never had. However, it didn't ease the ache of wanting nor make the melancholy of loss fade.

"Jane," he began but didn't finish. He rubbed the back of his neck with his palm as though unsure of what to say.

"Yes?" She fought hard to keep the hope from showing in her voice as she leaned back against the nearest bedpost. Her fingers curled in the crimson hangings. The fabric was cool and soft to the touch.

"I wanted to…" He finally met her gaze. "I wanted to thank you for the kiss. I haven't been kissed like that in many years. It shouldn't have happened though." He pushed away from the door, and after a moment, he walked toward her, a look of determination hardening his features momentarily. With his every step drawing him closer, her breath hitched, and she clung to the hangings for support. When he was mere inches away from her, he simply stared at her face and then focused on her mouth as though the answers he sought were there. She licked her lips nervously as sharp hunger spiked through her. Would he kiss her again? Would she lose herself anew in his embrace?

"Why?" she asked.

He ignored her question. "Who are you, Jane? Who are you really?" His whispered question made her shiver. She didn't know the answer herself. He trailed the back of his knuckles over her cheek, and another shiver rippled through her, like a pool of water disturbed by a stone cast into its depths.

"Who am I? I don't know…not anymore." She was Jane, but she wasn't Jane any longer. The more she was around him, the more she felt she was changing. Like the coastline by Sandsfoot Castle ruins, her sense of self was altering with the force of Bastian's presence, which pounded at her like mighty waves. They would shape and form each other and become something new, only she wasn't sure what that would be. She simply knew that she belonged with him, wherever he was.

But he didn't want her, wouldn't have anything to do with her. Every time he touched her, he reminded her it was wrong, that they shouldn't do it. Then why did he keep coming back to her? It didn't make any sense, and she knew logically she shouldn't want him either.

He lowered his head and feathered his lips along her jaw, and her lashes fluttered as pleasure and need fueled each other until her skin was burning.

"You are a mystery to me." His words rumbled against the sensitive skin of her neck as he pressed his body into hers, pinning her to the bedpost. "You're an American, but you act as though this place is in your blood. I see your love of my home shining in your eyes, even as you fear its darkness." He stole a brief, hot kiss before continuing. "You look like her, Jane. Did you know that? When I first saw you, I thought you were Isabelle come back from the dead."

His hands cupped her shoulders, fingers tensing. "I thought I'd gone mad, believing such nonsense, and then I gave in and kissed you, and we…" His mouth trembled as he kissed her again, this time deep but too brief. "It's as if the past is repeating itself …" He shook his head ruefully. "What does it matter? I want this. I want *you,* even though I shouldn't."

She opened her mouth to deny him, but no words were there. His mouth came down hard on hers, and she was caught in the tide and pulled away from the safety of the shore.

Isabelle. He thinks I look like Isabelle, and I think he looks like Richard. It was the only thought to penetrate the haze of her mind during that everlasting kiss. His hands never left her face, and his thumbs stroked her cheeks in a soothing rhythm. They focused only on that kiss and the infinite perfection of the way they moved together as though they'd kissed for a thousand years and would do so for a thousand more. His body pressed against hers in a small rocking motion that hypnotized her. A simple meeting of their mouths, and she came undone. A flick of his tongue against hers, the flash of unguarded emotion in his brown eyes.

When they finally parted and he met her gaze, their panting breaths shared the quiet air around them. She knew she would never be the same. She could never go back to her books and her research and not think of him.

What have I done? Fear slid through her, making her tremble. She didn't want him to have this power over her. The way she'd felt for Tim paled in comparison to the way Bastian made her feel and she'd only known him a matter of hours. What would Bastian do to her if she let him get inside her heart? She should want to be safe and free of him and the spell he wove around her, but she was caught in the gossamer strands of his web. But he'd already told her he didn't want anything to do with her—and if she told him about her dreams? He'd likely put her on the first flight to the U.S. as fast as he could get a staff member to take her to Heathrow.

"You're shaking," he murmured in concern and wrapped his arms around her, pulling her close. She tucked her face against his chest, inhaling his scent and bathing in his warmth. It was an awful weakness to want to be held and comforted, but she couldn't deny it, even knowing how dangerous it was to open herself up to him.

If someone had told her before she came here that within a day the Earl of Weymouth would be holding her in his arms, she would never have believed it. Yet here she was, letting him in where she swore no other man would be allowed. Suddenly all of her remaining energy vanished, and she collapsed, exhausted.

"Jane! Should I call the doctor?" His breathless tone made her insides warm, and she shook her head.

"I'm fine. I just need to sleep. It's been an insane day. Give me a few hours sleep, and I'll be as good as new." The lie felt heavy on her tongue. It was her heart that hurt, but she wouldn't dare tell him that. She pushed back from him a little and leaned back to sit on the bed.

"If you're sure you're all right…?" He didn't look convinced. His brows were lowered as he studied her from head to foot.

"Really, you should sleep, too. You're face is going to hurt tomorrow." She silently begged that he would leave her alone. A girl just wanted to curl into a ball and lick her wounds after rejection, not have a man gently comfort her. She wasn't in the mood to deal with mixed signals.

A ghost of a smile flitted across his face. "I fear you're right."

He returned to her door, and with one last look of concern he said, "Good night, Jane."

"Good night, Bastian." In that moment she felt safe and

protected, even after everything she had seen today.

"You know, I like that you call me Bastian." He chuckled, the sound so soft and inviting.

"You do?" It just occurred to her that she had forgotten her manners and did the American thing by consistently calling a peer of the English realm by his first name.

"Yes, I do. I don't feel so alone." This last comment was so quiet, she almost wondered if she had dreamed it. He closed the door behind him.

She stayed on the bed for a minute longer before she roused herself and went over to her suitcase. Dark stains made splotchy patterns on the red fabric of the bag. She laid it down and unzipped it. With a sigh of relief, she dug through the contents, finding nothing damaged. She found her flannel pajamas and changed into them and got into bed.

The fire in the hearth was lit beneath the painting. The logs crackled and snapped as they were consumed by the ravenous flames. Randolph must have lit the fire before he'd gone to bed. It warmed the room up and yet the dance of shadows made Jane uneasy. She snuggled deep into the comforter and willed herself to sleep. She wasn't sure how long it took, but just before she started to drift off, one of the shadows thickened into a strange shape…like a body hanging from a noose.

She blinked, and it was gone.

Just a dream. Please let it be a dream.

Chapter Seven

Bastian leaned back against the wall next to Jane's closed door. His body was rigid, tension coiled like snakes in his muscles. He had kissed her again, had almost lost control again. But she had tasted so good, like wine and her own natural sweetness. The way she had shivered and gasped, breathless as he held her, still echoed in his ears and made him ache bone deep to go back into her room and finish what he had started. Neither of them spoke about the drawing room incident or how they had been so intimate there yet like distant voyeurs. However, the kitchen and her bedroom...those two kisses belonged solely to them and not to the past.

They couldn't keep doing this, a dance circling closer and closer to each other until they made the mistake of sleeping together. It couldn't be allowed to happen. She didn't seem strong enough to stay away from him, so he would have to be the one to stop it. But damned if he hadn't been the one kissing her! He raked a hand through his hair, tugging hard on the strands in his desperation to think. Maybe if he chose to completely avoid her the rest of the week, then he could just send her packing and be done with it and they'd never cross paths again. Yes, that might work. Stormclyffe was large. He could easily avoid one little bookworm.

He pushed away from the wall, regret making his steps heavy, and his boots knocked into something.

A bag toppled over at his feet. Jane's briefcase. He started to pick it up when he noticed a leather-bound book with a blank spine lay on top of her notebook. It was old, not a textbook or research material. He knew he should just slide it inside the bag and leave it alone, but his hands were already curling around the tome and lifting it up. He hissed as an electric shock pulsed through his skin at his palms and fingers where he held the book. Rather than drop it, he suddenly found he couldn't let go of it. How could a book shock him? They didn't carry electric current…

It fell open, the yellowed paper parting soundlessly. Handwriting in faded ink flowed in delicate swirls and loops across the pages. Bastian's eyes widened as he read the first couple of lines.

This was his ancestor Richard's diary. How had Jane found this? Where had she found it? A part of him snarled. She had kept this a secret from him. He had every right to know what lay in the pages, to see the story his ancestor told. It was *his* family not hers, and he had expressly denied her access to his family's private papers. His fist was halfway raised in front of her door before he realized he was about to knock. He didn't want to quarrel with her. No. He would simply take the diary and protect it. She could come to him if she really wanted it. And she'd have to admit to him that she'd found it and was keeping it from him. If she wasn't brave enough to confront him, then he'd have the diary safe with him.

He crossed the hall and entered his own bedroom. It was a mirror of Jane's room, only with midnight-blue hangings around the bed, and it lacked a portrait over the fireplace of course. Instead there was a lovely mural of Stormclyffe Hall surrounded by the woods. Several black fallow deer were at the edge of the forest. They were beautiful creatures. There was a wild herd that had lived on the estate's lands for the last two-hundred-and fifty years. They weren't shy, and he had successfully hand-fed a few of them the first week he had moved in. The old groundskeeper he had hired to oversee the estate's lands had advised him on how to work with the deer.

He set the journal down on the bed, a little relieved that he could let go of the book that had clung to his hands like a magnet only a few seconds before. Then he went over to the tall armoire against one wall. The old wood creaked as he opened the door and retrieved his silk pajama bottoms. After stripping off his clothes, he donned the pants and turned around.

"Christ!" He nearly jumped at the sight of the diary on the bed.

It was lying open to a section in the middle. He'd been sure that when he had set the journal down it had been closed. He strode over to the bed, and flipped it shut and then, experimenting, he pressed the bed down next to the book. Bastian wasn't sure what he expected, maybe that the book would flip open due to a dipping spot in the mattress.

The book didn't move.

The fine hairs on his arm stood on end, and a cool breeze teased him from behind as though some cold beast from the far north breathed down the back of his neck. He knew if Jane was here, she would mention ghosts and hauntings. He didn't want to entertain that possibility. He picked up the journal, closed it, and just stared at the cover. What did he expect? To suddenly see visions or hear the voice of a man long dead? He shook his head when nothing happened. Jane was having a bad influence on him. Still…there was no harm in browsing a few pages. The book became heavy in his hands, and when he loosened his hold, it parted again to that same spot. He began to read.

June 1st 1810

I can't escape her. She is hounding my every step. Cordelia Huntington and her father have developed a habit of appearing whenever I go to town. Whenever I attend any social function, they are there. I've seen many a woman watch me with interest and desire, but the way Cordelia eyes me, in a strangely possessive way like a cat eyeing a mouse, is unnerving.

The whispering has started. Witchcraft. There have been cattle dying in town with no visible cause. And birds. So many birds, their little hearts ripped from their chests as their bodies appear outside of doorways, like some portent of doom. My days are filled with handling the concerns of my people and reassuring them that we have no witches in our town, even though I am not entirely sure if that is true. There's only one thing I want. To be with Isabelle. I cannot find a moment alone with her, the woman I crave beyond reason.

Today, though, today I was lucky. Her father and mother joined me as I escorted her to see the ruins of Sandsfoot Castle, an old structure that dates back to Henry VIII. As long as the visitors stay safely away from the more dangerous parts of the shore, which could easily crumble, it is a safe spot for picnics and outings. I knew it was to be the perfect spot to propose to Isabelle.

As I waited outside Braxton's inn, I shifted restlessly in the seat of my carriage, my fingers curling around my mother's garnet ring, which was tucked safely in my waistcoat pocket. My footman appeared at the door, opening it and assisting the waiting guests inside. Mr. and Mrs. Braxton climbed in, taking the seats opposite me. The innkeeper and his wife were all smiles and warmth, something I liked immensely about them.

They were genuine people and did not try to befriend me out of any desire to climb a social ladder.

Isabelle's face appeared as she peeked into the coach. Her beautiful eyes lit up when she saw me, and she smiled. My body burst into flames inside. She was so lovely, but it isn't merely her looks which held me in rapture. It is her kindness, her intelligence, and the hint of passion she tries to hide each time upon our meeting. Last evening, we danced again, and my hand fit to her waist perfectly. A high color had blossomed in her cheeks, and I knew then that we would enjoy lovemaking. The night couldn't come soon enough. I wanted to please her, to give her so much, my life, my love, my soul, my passion. I wanted her to own me. A man shouldn't want to admit to such a desire, I know, but it's true. I wish for her to brand her name upon my heart and never leave me.

She slipped inside the coach and sat next to me before I could even get out and hand her in.

"Thank you for this lovely outing, my lord," Mr. Braxton said.

"You are most welcome," I answered, and I meant it.

The weather was perfect for the picnic. The attending footman saw to it the drinks and food were prepared and laid out on several blankets. The wicker baskets were overflowing with cold roast, boiled eggs, and shortbread. My footman, George, stood by ready to refill our glasses with lemonade or Madeira wine. Isabelle's parents occupied one blanket while Isabelle and I occupied the other.

As always, I engaged Mr. Braxton in a frank and intelligent discussion. Despite the other man's humble beginnings, he was well spoken and very bright. He was much the opposite of a man like Sir Huntington who did not care to know the most basic of intellectual subjects but instead preferred to bandy about names and titles of people whom he could curry favor with. The Braxtons were a far cry from that part of my life, and

I relished any chance to escape such social engagements that would bring me into close quarters with the Huntingtons.

After we had finished eating, I politely got Mr. Braxton's attention.

"Could I be allowed to take Miss Braxton on a walk closer to the ruins?"

Isabelle sat up a little straighter on our blanket, her gaze darted between me and her father, the glimmer of hope barely concealed in her eyes. Did she know of my plan to propose? Surely not, I've kept the secret so guarded, she could not know.

"Yes, of course," Mr. Braxton replied, a soft and yet knowing glint in his eyes.

I offered Isabelle my hand and assisted her in standing. We strolled along the green path toward the cliffs, her arm tucked in mine. Another confession had to be made, and I feared weaker men would think it made me a fool. But the pleasure of having Isabelle's hand resting lightly upon my arm as we walked in amiable silence was one of the best moments of my life. When we were only a few yards away from the ruins, I stopped and clasped Isabelle's hands in mine.

For a few moments, she kept her gaze on the ruins. "It's peaceful here." She sighed and turned to look my way.

My heart pounded as I struggled to find the words I had rehearsed a dozen times this morning.

"Isabelle, we have only known each other a few weeks, but in that short time I have come to regard your company greatly." I swallowed, hoping to speak around the sudden knot in my throat. Sweat dewed on my forehead, and I prayed I could be strong enough to ask her. If she refused me…I could not think of that. I decided I had to continue.

Something sad filled her eyes, darkening the gray luminescence to a shadow-stormy blue.

"I know what you must say," she interjected when I would have spoken. Her tone was gentle, and her eyes brimmed with

a sadness I hoped never to see in her.

"You do?" Did she mean to reject me?

"Yes. You must, of course. We cannot go on as we are. It's better to end things."

"I must what?" I stumbled over her words. "End things?" I shook my head almost violently and raised her hands to my lips, feverishly kissing them. "No, no, that's not it at all, my love. I was going to propose to you. If you will let me."

I tried to tease her, but she stared at me in confusion.

"Propose? To me?" Her voice rose an octave. "But you must marry someone of your station. I am nobody. An innkeeper's daughter."

The scorn for her station was evident in every syllable. It pained me she thought so little of herself. I wished she saw herself the way I always had.

"I don't care, Isabelle. I want you. Would you prefer me to go to London and marry a simpering bore? Isabelle," I groaned in exasperation. "You!" I kissed her hands again. "You are the only woman I want and need. Please."

I dropped to one knee and retrieved the ring from my pocket and offered it to her. My heart thrashed against my ribs as I waited for her to react. "Please…please do me the honor of being my wife."

She looked away from me, her eyes drinking in the castle ruins and the sea beyond before she returned her gaze to me. When she did, tears streaked down her face.

"Why do you weep, my heart?" I surged to my feet and wrapped my arms around her. Every time we touched, lightning seemed to strike my body and bind me tighter to her. She had to say yes, had to agree to end my torment. I kept the ring cupped in my palm.

"I'm overcome with happiness, my lord." Her words were breathless and hitched as though she fought off the urge to cry.

I stared at her, hope filling me with a secret warmth. "Does *that mean you plan to accept my offer?"*

I lifted the ring up, watching the way it reflected in her eyes like a shining star.

She held out her left hand. "Yes. A thousand times, yes."

I could barely breathe. My blood thudded in my ears like a stallion across the moors as I slid the garnet ring over Isabelle's finger.

"Oh, Richard, whatever shall we do? The gossips in town will never let us go through with this. We will be shunned."

"Shunned? No. We will not. I'm the earl. You will be my countess. The people can think what they will, but you will have the respect owed to you as my wife."

"I don't care about that." Isabelle's fingertips traced my jaw and my lips. "I only want you to be happy." It was true, every word. Only she mattered; only her joy and love meant anything to me.

I grinned, playful and excited. She was mine; we would be together and be happy.

"The only reason for living is to be with you. You make me happy." I lifted her chin and bent to kiss her. It was everything I had imagined it would be. She gave in to her own desire for me and wrapped her arms around my shoulders, tugging me closer.

"We will be so happy, my love." It was our first kiss, but it would not be our last, not for many years yet, I hoped.

Chapter Eight

Bastian let the journal fall to his lap. His eyes burned, and his throat was tight. He almost felt he had been there, the sea breeze playing with his hair as he kissed the only woman he would ever love, never knowing he would lose her in just a short while. Barely a year later, Isabelle would be dead, and Richard would follow her to the grave a few months afterward.

Goose bumps covered his arms. He flipped the journal closed and set it on the nightstand. He didn't know what to think. The story of his ancestors' lives filled these pages. Details of Isabelle's death might be in here somewhere. No wonder Jane had ferreted the diary away. It was the perfect primary source for her dissertation. As a fellow historian, he knew its value and had to acknowledge the truth—that not letting her have this would hurt her research. The last thing he wished to do was hurt Jane.

But if he gave her this, it would open the door to his family's darkest secrets. Could he do that? Sacrifice the protection of his family in order to give Jane what she needed to finish her paper? If he didn't, she would lose the support of her committee chair on her topic and wouldn't get her PhD. He didn't want to be the person who stood in the way of her dreams.

She was a woman lost and doing her best to find a place that was hers. He understood that feeling all too well. Stormclyffe Hall was his refuge. Even though the place was shrouded in tragedy and its stones soaked with innocent blood, it was still the one place that was truly his. London had never felt the way the castle did. He loved the feel of the cold stone beneath his bare feet and the slightly salty taste to the air from the sea. This was his home. Perhaps it was Jane's, too.

A laugh escaped his lips at the rogue thought. Jane, living here. What a foolish idea. It didn't make any sense. She was a student at Cambridge, with a life there, and eventually she would return to America.

He eyed the journal ruefully and then got back out of bed. He took the book, went back out into the hall, slipping it back into Jane's briefcase. When he straightened, he heard a voice, muffled voice on the other side of Jane's doors. Ears straining, he listened to the sounds.

"No! No don't leave me! Please, I cannot do this alone." The voice belonged to Jane, but it was so full of despair and fear that he didn't hesitate to act. He burst into her room. The meager light from the hall split a path in the darkness by the bed and revealed Jane thrashing wildly, her limbs tangled fretfully in her sheets.

"No!" she wailed sharply, and then her body seized violently.

"Jane." He dashed to the bed and grabbed hold of her, dragging her coiled body into his arms. She slackened in his hold almost instantly and didn't wake right away. He stroked the wild, dark waves of hair back so he could see her face. Her lashes fluttered like an injured hummingbird's wings, and then she finally looked at him.

"What happened?" Her voice was hoarse as though she had been screaming for hours.

"You were shouting in your sleep." He delivered the news gently, not wanting to frighten her further, but he hoped she would explain what had happened.

"I was?" She moved slightly, her body sliding against his. His groin tightened, and he held her closer as a wave of longing swept through him. He needed to let go of her. Any more of this and he'd give into his need to kiss her again. *Distance. Must keep my distance.*

One of her hands laid flat on his bare chest, the tips of her fingers were stiff and dug into his skin, like a kitten clinging to its mother. He couldn't easily disentangle himself from her now, so he surrendered to the desire to soothe her.

"Were you dreaming?" His hands traveled down her back, soothing her with slow massaging touches.

"I think so." She settled into him more, resting her cheek on his chest. That single point of skin-to-skin contact frayed his control.

He lightly pressed his palms into her lower back, and she stretched out on her bed and allowed herself to be tucked into his side. The position felt natural, as though he had done it a thousand times with Jane. It was so easy to be with her. He barely knew her, yet the press of her body to his eased the restlessness that always gripped him. In recent years, he had stalked from bed to bed of every beautiful woman he came across, refusing to linger with any one woman. Jane rooted him to the spot, like a sapling that had finally found a bed of earth deep and rich enough to support him. And he was going to lose her. She would leave at the end of the week, and he would never see her again. *For my family's sake, I have to let you go.* The mere thought of it made his stomach twist.

Mine. She belongs to me. She cannot leave. The voice that growled in the back of his head was not his own, but he had the urge to agree with it.

"Do you remember what you were dreaming about?" he asked, mentally pushing the strange voice aside.

He felt her give a little nod against his chest.

"I was following a woman in a white nightgown. She was running through the castle. There were shadows everywhere."

"Did you catch up to her?"

She licked her lips. "Yes. She stopped in front of an old dovecote. When I got to her, she pointed at the ground, and all around her there were doves. *Dead doves*. Their little hearts ripped from their snowy-white breasts. The woman turned to me and she—"

"She what?" he prompted. His heartbeat pounded against his temples.

"She said, 'By innocence bled beneath pale moonlight, the evil one has begun to fight. Touch not the heart of evil. Trust not the shadows. What once was broken must be mended.' Then she was gone."

Every bone in Bastian's body seemed to burn. He blinked as a violent pain tore through him and just as quickly it was gone. His grandmother's voice rang in his ears. It was her warning. The one Jane knew somehow and now had dreamed about.

"Jane—"

"I'm sorry I had a nightmare and woke you up." She attempted to extricate herself from his hold, her cheeks red as she suddenly seemed to realize they had been cuddled together in her bed. He wasn't ashamed of his near nakedness, but she was certainly aware of it. Her gaze traveled the length of his body, stilling on his bare chest for several seconds before she cleared her throat and turned her focus back to his face. A little grimace replaced her bashfulness. "You need rest. Your face…it looks like it hurts."

Instinctively, she moved her hands up to his face and

brushed over the tender flesh. "It doesn't matter. It was just a bad dream."

She looked away from him. "What if I told you it was more than just a bad dream? That I've been having these sort of nightmares for a few years?"

"I think they're just dreams, Jane. Try to relax."

She scowled at him, but there was hurt and betrayal in her eyes at his dismissal. It couldn't be helped though. Better that she be angry with him than if she started to care for him.

Bastian swept his hands back around her waist, trying to draw her back down. He needed to have her lying next to him.

She bit her lip and resisted. "I don't think this is a good idea. This is all too…" She waved a hand in the air in a helpless gesture.

He grasped her chin and angled it so she had to face him. "I've lived my life on bad ideas, and it hasn't failed me yet." He pulled her down and enfolded her in his arms. "Don't think about tomorrow, Jane, none of it. It's just you and me right now. Focus on that, and you will be fine." Her muscles relaxed and she ceased her resistance.

The fire still burned in the hearth, and Bastian lay awake, watching the logs turn to white ash before he sensed Jane's breathing lighten. She was sleeping at last.

Please, let her have no more nightmares.

The sound and sight of her fear had forced a primal, protective instinct forward in him. With each little harm she suffered, it felt as though he suffered, too. He slid one of his hands into her hair, threading his fingers through the dark, silky strands. A throaty little purr escaped Jane, and she cuddled closer. In that moment there was no place he wanted to be but here in bed with his charming little bookworm who jumped at shadows and dreamed of women dressed in white. He didn't know a thing about her, not anything he could claim by words alone, but he did know her somehow. Like a half-remembered dream that faded come dawn until it was only a memory of a sensation, a whisper of words, or a fleeting image from the corner of his eye.

"Who are you, Jane? I must know," he murmured as the last embers of the fire perished and darkness reigned.

• • •

Her body was heaven. Nothing existed beyond her wild cries of pleasure and the pulse of fire that leaped in his own veins. Lost in a crimson haze of hungry passion, he devoured the sweetness of her mouth and sank into the most secret part of her body and soul until their essences seemed to become one being, not two. Their hands met above their heads, and he twined his fingers through hers, even as he kept her trapped beneath him. She was forced to surrender the control of their lovemaking, but he would see to it that this moment was everything she had ever dreamed of.

"My heart," he growled against the soft skin of her neck and thrust hard into her. She quaked beneath him, her hips rising as she sought to get closer to his body.

"As you are mine." Her breathless reply stung his senses and tenderness flooded his chest in a warm wave of satisfied longing. There could never be heaven anywhere else but where she was. He would have captured the moon and stolen a constellation of stars to lay at her feet if it would make her smile even once. No man had ever been so blessed as he was.

The passion and desire built like a steady blaze between them until there was no stopping, no slowing down, only the rush to the glorious end.

"Isabelle!" His lips broke apart with his cry, and every bit of strength failed him as he released his soul into her. Her own stifled scream of joy was throaty and thick with sated pleasure. He laid his head upon her breasts, gasping for breath. Her

hand smoothed his hair back from his face as she softly panted beneath him. The intimacy of it was so wondrous that he felt like a young boy riding a horse for the first time across the sloping hills. He was free, but not alone. Isabelle was with him. Always. Forever.

Bastian woke with a start, his head pounding, his throat tight as he fought off a shout of despair. His chest was empty as though a thief had slipped a hand between his ribs and stolen his heart. A desperate longing filled that void with leaden weights, and for a second, he couldn't breathe.

The dream. It was just that, a dream. He had dreamed of Isabelle and making love to her. A shudder racked him, and he cuddled Jane's warm body closer. Was he a mad man or a fool for wishing the dream had been reality and it had been Jane who was his, sharing her passion with him? A cold sense of dread trespassed along his spine. She was not his, could never be his, and yet holding her like this was sheer devastation to him.

After Richard and Isabelle, the women who fell in love with the men of Stormclyffe always died, which was what had led to the myth of the Weymouth curse. Except his mother. Her life had been spared, whereas his father had died. Witnesses had reported to the papers that a woman had been seen near the crash, a woman in white, wandering along the deserted road. It had led to a frenzy of ghost stories. Time and time again, people had whispered that his father had risked his own life by coming back to the deserted castle all those years ago in order to trade his life for his wife's to the dark fates that held the Carlisle family captive.

It was bad luck to have someone here purposely exposing his family history. And Jane, even with all her academic credentials, was still no better than a paparazzo with a pen rather than camera.

If Bastian had any sense, any real strength, he would slip

out of this bed and leave her now before his feelings for her deepened beyond redemption. He was not his ancestor, and Jane was not Isabelle. He had no claim to the woman in his arms, and she had none to him, but Christ, he wanted it more than his next breath.

A sudden wellspring of hope roared through him with the force of a mighty gale. There was nothing to stop him from taking her and running to the ends of the earth to escape his family's reputation. He could seduce her blind, sweep her off her feet, and never let her go. A hundred faces of women he'd been with all faded whenever he thought of Jane. They had been empty entertainments, mere phantoms compared to his Jane.

Was this how it had been for Richard? The undeniable pull, like planets to the sun, to be with this one woman? A passion stronger than any of society's laws, a love deeper than the northern seas. There was no turning back, no walking away from emotions like that once he set down that path. Did he love Jane? No, not yet, but—

Jane stirred restlessly before settling back to sleep. Soon dawn would come, and he would show her his world. A world he wanted to share.

Soon.

Chapter Nine

The empty bed woke Jane the following morning. It was as if Bastian's absence had jarred her body awake. She didn't know whether to laugh bitterly or shake her head. Last night she and Bastian had shared a bed, and she had loved every minute of it. And now he was gone. Again. Hot and cold. The man could write a book on leaving women confused. Of course, she was becoming the queen of mixed signals herself. Hadn't she clung to him like she was drowning? Bastian probably couldn't have escaped her death grip last night until she'd fallen to sleep. The image of him prying her fingers off his body wasn't a flattering one.

She rolled onto her back, watching the gold beams of light through the half-pulled-back crimson moreen hangings. Birds twittered outside. The sound of their chatter was comforting. She loved birds. There had always been birds back home. It was something she missed when she spent time in London. Sure there were plenty of pigeons, but nothing replaced wild birdsong. She and Tim used to lie in bed late on Saturdays, listening to birds and the beat of each other's hearts. Tears pricked her eyes, and she blinked them away.

It was no surprise Bastian had fled her bedroom. She'd confessed about the dreams last night, and he'd cut her off before she could fully explain. He obviously thought she was crazy, just like Tim had. Would she ever find a man who would believe her? Regret and shame turned her stomach into knots.

Why couldn't I keep my mouth shut?

But it had been so easy to talk to Bastian, to tell him everything that was in her heart and to share her fears.

The door swung open, and she sat upright. Bastian entered, nudging the door open farther with his foot as he carried a tray inside. A delightful breakfast of eggs, toast, and bacon adorned with a bright bouquet of wildflowers was presented to her with the solemnity and grandeur owed to a queen. A blush worked its way across her face, and her heart gave a treacherous little flutter of joy. He hadn't abandoned her. She did not miss the mischievous twinkle in his warm brown eyes.

"Breakfast. I wanted to spare Randolph the stairs this morning. He gets a touch of rheumatism from time to time." He set the tray down over her lap and then eased down on the edge of the bed next to her, leaning back against the pillows beside her in a pose of utter relaxation.

Trying to ignore the intimacy of the moment, she spoke up. "What about you? Have you eaten?" She was already reaching for the plate of toast to offer him a slice. She wanted to ask him about his original plan to avoid her; it had been such an obvious goal yesterday. Yet here he was, bringing her breakfast. The last time she'd questioned his intentions toward her, he'd shut down completely. She'd stay quiet if it kept him here and happy.

He shook his head and patted his stomach. "Already ate. I had a quick bite after I showered."

Even though it was covered by a light gray sweater, she

remembered too vividly the washboard abs beneath. She also remembered she'd kept her hand on those ropes of muscled steel half the night. The memory singed her insides.

He seemed to realize that he was lounging on her bed like a jungle cat, and suddenly recovered some of his manners. Sliding off the bed, he grinned sheepishly. "I'll leave you to your meal. Let me know when you are ready for the tour."

"Right, the tour. Thanks." She was blushing, with no reason for it, but damn it, she was. It wasn't like he would take her on the tour. Poor Randolph had that chore.

He paused by her bedpost at the foot of the bed, rapping his knuckles lightly as he hesitated. "How did you sleep?"

She blinked and dropped her toast. It knocked the knife off the plate and onto the tray with a loud clatter.

"Sleep? I…"

"I mean the nightmares. No more of them, I hope?"

"Oh no, no more. Thank you…" She could practically feel her face turning red again. "Thank you for staying with me. I'm not a scaredy-cat. I swear I don't hop on chairs when I see mice or anything. It's just…well…I believe this stuff. Stupid, I know. But I do believe." She waited for him to accuse of her being insane, the way Tim had when she'd tried to tell him about how vivid her nightly dreams had become. Bastian didn't do that.

He nodded slowly.

For a moment she couldn't think. He'd changed since last night, and seemed more open, less torn by dark thoughts she couldn't hear. Why?

Then he winked, and she reacted instantly and impishly threw a flower from the plate at him. He ducked, and the thick blossom sailed over his head.

"Fair enough." He laughed. The sound warmed her right down to her toes and yet it hurt at the same time because it was too good to be true and was sure not to last. He headed for the door and closed it behind him as he left.

Her stomach turned, and an emptiness settled in her like a dead weight. Every time he left, something in her seemed to go deathly still, like she was trapped beneath a frozen lake, holding her breath until it hurt. She had warned herself to be careful around him, and yet her attraction to him was inevitable, as though her path to him had been written in the stars eons ago.

It would never work; there were too many problems. She suffered night terrors about his family home and refused to trust a man with her heart and her strange dreams and their connection to the past. He wanted nothing to do with anyone who believed in the Weymouth curse and seemed completely undone by her flashes of clairvoyance. Even if they could get past those surmountable issues, she was American, still knee-deep in her studies. He was a titled peer from a dying noble line. They were at different points in their lives. They made no sense on paper.

But when their hands brushed and lips met…a deep burn moved through her like the flowing of lava. It changed her in ways that were permanent; *he* had changed her. He made her want things, made her desire to live a life of passion and intensity, one outside her books and studies. Her careful, quiet life was undone by his kiss. A little shiver flushed her skin in a smattering of goose bumps, and she forced herself to eat her breakfast.

After a fast shower, she dressed in a cream wool sweater, light brown pants, and a pair of old riding boots from her equestrian days in college. They were snug but warm and perfect for marching around gardens and fields. As she meandered down the hall toward Bastian's study, she combed her fingers through her hair, hoping she looked all right. Randolph had been nowhere in sight, so she might have to have Bastian point her to where she was going to meet the butler for the tour.

She paused at his study door, noticing it was ajar. Soft strains of classic seventies rock music filled the air. Her lips twitched. The man and his music. She couldn't blame him. Some of the best songs came from the likes of The Doors and Jimi Hendrix. After placing a palm on the worn wood surface of the door, she pushed it open.

The study was, in a word, perfect. A laptop sat on a polished Chippendale desk covered in papers. Bastian sat in the desk chair, his back to the door as he worked. A fire crackled in a stone fireplace opposite the desk. On either side were two tall, dark wooden bookshelves filled with books, both ancient and new. A portrait of a man and woman holding hands and sharing a love seat peered at her from the gilded frame above the fireplace. The man and woman both resembled Bastian.

His parents. It had to be. Their clothes were modern, and the pose was sweet and romantic. Her heart fractured a little at the sight, knowing that such a love had been ended by Bastian's father's death. No wonder his mother wouldn't come here, not if this place held such a wealth of painful memories.

Bastian hadn't seemed to notice she'd opened the door. He shuffled some papers on his desk and tucked them away before turning back to a spreadsheet on his computer. She'd taken two steps inside before the tip of her boot caught on something lying near the door and she stumbled.

"Oompf!" Her palms smacked the stone floor as she broke her fall.

"Jane?" He spun on his swivel chair and took stock of her sprawled on the floor. He reached for her, helping her up and brushing her off.

"Sorry, I tripped over..." She glanced down at a pair of worn brown wing-tip shoes. They were large, but not quite as big as Bastian's. She scrutinized the shoes carefully, they were unpolished and old-looking.

"Are these yours?" She pointed at the shoes.

Bastian immediately bent and picked them up, his hold protective and impossibly gentle as he set them on his desk.

"They were my father's." He rubbed at a light scratch on the left shoe's toe and then with a sigh he stepped away from them.

She didn't press him, but she sensed there was something important about them. He gestured for her to sit in one of the two wingback chairs opposite his desk.

"They were his favorite pair. Mother begged him to get a new pair, but he used to laugh and say, 'Sweetheart, when something was made just for you, you should never let it go.' Her eyes used to shine after he said that, and it wasn't until I was older I realized he wasn't just talking about the shoes."

A sad expression darkened his eyes, and he gazed far away as though lost in bittersweet memories.

"Why did you mother remain in London?" she asked, even though she could guess the answer.

"This place scares her. My father died on the very road we drove last night. They found his car in a ditch the next morning." Bastian's face had turned ashen as he spoke, and Jane regretted asking him. Some pains were too deep to relive and survive.

"He was hoping to come back here and restore it. After he died, my mother refused to even mention Stormclyffe."

And then Jane understood. The last piece of his puzzle fell into place. Bastian was trying to do what his father had wanted. Restore the ancestral home. Complete his father's dream at any cost. It must have been a way for him to connect to his lost parent. Her gaze lingered on the worn pair of wing tips. A brush of warmth teased her face, as though someone had touched her cheek. Unlike the other frightening encounters she'd had in the castle, this moment was safe. A soothing, protective presence seemed to emanate from the general direction of the shoes. Oddly, the memory of that gardener she'd met yesterday came back to her. She'd felt the same way around him.

She reached reflexively for her necklace. Bastian leaned into her, catching the chain with his index finger and placing his other hand on the back of her chair behind her right shoulder.

"I showed you mine. Now you show me yours." He used his finger to slide the necklace out of her sweater. Her own fingers were still locked around the medallion. It was so personal, this part of her, yet she owed it to him to share with him. He let go of her chair and leaned back against his desk, his long legs crossed at the ankles and his palms resting on the edge of the desk.

"It was my grandmother's," she said. "When she was sixteen she was in a car accident with her older brother. They declared her dead on the scene and rushed him to the hospital. She was taken straight to the morgue since they thought she was already dead and they had to get her brother in surgery. The hospital staff in those days weren't as knowledgeable as they are now, and her heartbeat slowed down so much and was so faint that they'd thought she was gone. She woke up there a few hours later, terrified, but alive…"

Jane shut her eyes, awash with memories of Nonnie, the beautiful old woman who spun stories like tapestries.

"Nonnie told me about how when she was unconscious from the accident, she dreamed of a man with wings of light who slayed dragons. It made a lasting impression on her. When she was eighteen, she traveled to France and visited a monastery. She had this medallion blessed there." Jane opened her eyes and lifted the silver pendant up so he could see it.

"It's the archangel Michael slaying a serpent. She gave it to me when I turned seventeen and received my confirmation at church. I rarely take it off. It makes me feel…" She hesitated.

"Safe," he said.

"Yeah. I know it sounds foolish."

"No more foolish than me carrying around a pair of my father's shoes. To each his own." Bastian flashed her a genuine smile, not one of seduction or sadness, but simply a warm smile, one a friend would give. Were they friends? Could they be friends? She wanted them to be. Honestly, she wanted them to be more than that, but she couldn't afford to think about it.

"Bastian, can we talk? Truthfully?" She held her breath, praying he'd agree.

A little sigh escaped him, and he nodded.

"What really happened in the drawing room when we first met? I mean, why do you think it happened? We went at each other like crazy, and we'd never met before."

His stare moved to a spot on the wall above her head. "What do you think happened?"

"Honestly? I feel like something possessed me. It was all so distant in my head, and my body was just happily going along with the sensations. That's never happened to me before."

"Me neither. I also felt…distant, as though a puppet on strings. Please don't take offense, it was fantastic, what we did, but the other times we…kissed…that was different. Infinitely more than what happened in the drawing room. Does that make sense?" He looked down at her again, his gaze searching.

"Yeah, the other times were amazing, beyond amazing. Do you think we were possessed, in the drawing room I mean?" It was the only thing that made sense, as scared as she was to consider the possibility.

"I don't really believe in that sort of thing but…"

"But?"

"Maybe there is a weight to your unusual connection to

Stormclyffe, to me." He shoved away from his desk and held out his hand. "Let's not talk about it any more today. You have a tour to take and a dissertation to write. Come with me." He led her away from the study, and the flickering sense of warmth flooded her before it was gone.

"Are we going to meet Randolph?"

He shook his head. "I changed my mind. I'll be taking you around the house today."

She arched a brow. "I thought you had important things to do?"

"I still do, but this is my house, and you are my guest. It occurred to me that I should treat you as such."

She let the matter lie, even though she wanted to question him and demand to know why he was putting himself in a situation that would bring them closer.

He led her down a set of stairs and into the old servants' quarters on the first floor, which had belonged to the butler and housekeeper. From there he led her to a Gothic archway with a heavy wooden door. Several pairs of boots and umbrellas were nestled in a medieval cloister style rack near the door. Dust lined the wood and stone, but this particular part of Stormclyffe felt lived in. Black-and-white pictures of the castle's grounds covered the wall opposite the umbrellas.

"My grandfather's. He wanted to be a photographer. He ended up running the estate instead, but he left these photographs as a memory of what could have been. Sometimes I think this place is a graveyard of broken dreams," he mused as he searched the coat rack. He found a brown canvas barn jacket with red flannel lining for Jane before he slipped on his own black peacoat.

"Your grandfather had a lot of talent. These are beautiful." She nodded at the pictures. "It's so sad he couldn't pursue his dream."

"It is," he agreed.

"Sometimes people have to sacrifice the things they love the most in order to do what they must to help those they care about." Her observation struck him deep. At his most unguarded moments, that was how he felt with her here. That if there were a Weymouth curse, he had to protect her against it. Like the other women the previous earls had…cared for.

They stepped out onto a vast stone balcony about ten feet above the ground. About thirty feet ahead, the stones cut off where a stone railing with two large urns on either side held planted flowers. Short staircases on the left and right sides offered access to the open fields ahead of them. She froze, her entire body caught up in strong sense of déjà vu. Beyond the balcony was a view of the sea. In the distance, storm clouds prowled low on the horizon. They would likely reach landfall in a few hours. The sun was still shining strong, and it warmed her face. Bastian lightly touched the small of her back, and she met his gaze.

"This way." He ushered her down the steps, and they started off across the field toward the forest.

When they arrived at the edge of the wood, he made several odd clicking noises with his teeth and reached into his jacket pocket. He uncurled his closed fingers, and she saw a handful of sugar cubes.

"What are these for?"

"You'll see." His rich laugh was soft and made her think of last night in her bedroom.

He continued to make the odd clicking noises, and suddenly, black shapes emerged from the trees straight ahead.

"What are they?" she whispered, clutching his arm.

"They're black fallow deer. They're relatively tame." His whisper danced through the air like a softly spoken spell. A large buck strode toward them, his antlered head held high, his dark eyes surveying them empirically as he seemed to debate whether they were worth the risk of drawing closer.

Finally, he gave in, snorting and stamping as he approached, and his nose nuzzled Bastian's open palm and the buck stole a couple of sugar cubes.

"He's beautiful." She sighed, lost in the dark magic of the creature before her.

"The herd has been here over two hundred years. Can you believe that?" He was gazing at the pair of does, which were delicately picking their way across the grass toward them. She felt enraptured by his look of childlike wonder.

God, he was handsome, but in that moment he was so much more than that. He was real, not an illusion or a dream. Something stirred inside her, and a question was upon her lips before she even had time to think about it.

"Bastian, when did you decide to come back here and restore Stormclyffe?"

He turned his attention away from the deer, and they vanished into the woods like black ghosts.

"April twenty-first, six years ago," he replied without hesitation as though the date were burned in his mind.

She sucked in a shocked breath, and the cold air burned her lungs. No…it couldn't be. The same day that Isabelle and Richard first met two hundred years before. And the same day and year she'd first seen a picture of Stormclyffe Hall. She wouldn't forget that date ever, because it marked the start of her nightmares. The memory was still vivid. She'd been tucked deep in the undergraduate library stacks her freshman year, sneezing from the dust and losing herself in primary source materials.

It had been early one morning, and no one else was there, so when a soft little *thunk* came from behind her, she'd turned and there it was. A book had fallen off a shelf, landing at her feet, pages splayed open to a black-and-white picture of the castle on the cliff side. She took one look and knew her life would never be the same.

"What is it, Jane?" His hands settled on her shoulders, and he captured her focus, dragging her from her memories.

"That's the day I saw the first picture of Stormclyffe and decided to research it."

His brows arched in surprise. "Please tell me you're joking."

She shook her head. "No, I'm not. And it's also the same day that Richard and Isabelle met…" She trailed off, and the pit of her stomach dropped as she realized her mistake. The diary. He didn't know about the diary or the day his ancestors met.

"How do you know that?" His eyes narrowed, and his hands dropped from her shoulders down to her waist.

She swore she saw his mouth twitch, as if he were trying not to laugh, which made no sense. She tried frantically to backpedal.

"I…uh…must have read it somewhere."

He bit his bottom lip, the evidence of a barely concealed smile so obvious now. He looked like a cat that had feasted on a canary and was eyeing the smattering of yellow feathers lying in front of his paws with satisfaction.

"Perhaps you read it say…in a journal?" His hands tightened on her waist as he urged her closer to him. Merriment danced in his eyes.

She jabbed an accusatory finger at his chest.

"You know! How did you find out?"

"I may or may not have found it when I knocked over your briefcase in the hall last night."

Her face burned, and she bowed her head. She had stolen it for all intents and purposes and should feel guilty, even if she intended to give it back when she was done.

"I planned to tell you I found it. I just wanted to read it first, in case you took it away from me." It was the truth.

"It's fine, Jane. I put it back in your bag. You're welcome

to use it, on two conditions." The sly look in his eyes should have been a warning.

"Oh? What are they?"

"You share with me whatever information you find out." He ticked off his first demand with one finger.

"And?"

"And…" He pulled her flush against him and slanted his mouth over hers.

Chapter Ten

The kiss was drugging, deep, and full of heat. His hands wandered and hers explored as she let him steal the kiss. He made it so easy to forget the world and just surrender to sensations. She wasn't sure how long they stayed like that, making out like teenagers desperate to get as much out of it as possible before one of them had the good sense to end it.

Cold little pricks stung her face and hands. Startled, she and Bastian broke apart as rain started to fall heavily around them. The clouds had rushed inland and opened up overhead. He grasped her hand and tugged her across the field.

"Come on, there's shelter ahead."

The rain-slicked grass made it difficult to run, and soon they were stumbling and laughing as they raced through the gardens. He led her down the path bordered by tall hedges, then took an abrupt right turn. Lightning laced the skies around them, and the only shelter nearby emerged in front of them. A dovecote. It was an octagonal building covered with ivy and roses. The thatched roof was solid and well kept despite its age. Thunder snarled around them like a pack of hungry wolves as they sprinted toward the structure. He grasped a wrought-iron handle and wrenched the door open. They stumbled into the darkness, and he closed the door behind them. The room was musty and smelled faintly of decaying roses. Tiny splinters of light came through the dove nesting holes at the top of the cupola.

She shivered, her wet hair plastered to her face. Bastian slicked his own hair back before reaching for her and enfolding her in his arms. With one hand, he tucked her head beneath his chin and just cradled her in his arms. God, it felt good. When was the last time she'd just been held? Tim hadn't been much of a holder. She'd missed this though, the intimacy of a man with his arms around her. The last six months had been so cold and lonely, but she'd been safe from heartache. She burrowed closer to Bastian, relishing his heat and how wonderful he made such intimacy feel but dreading knowing it would have to end. They couldn't keep doing this. One of them would break and give in and get hurt, and she would have bet her life that it would be her.

"Bastian?"

"Hmm?" He smoothed his hands over her back, and his cheek rubbed the top of her head.

"This looks like the place in my dream from last night." Worry knotted inside her stomach as she waited for his reaction.

"When you mentioned the dovecote, I wondered if it was here. You must have seen it in a picture."

She shook her head, breathing in his woodsy scent mixed with fresh rain. An addictive smell.

"No. I would have remembered. There aren't any pictures of the gardens in any of the books, because the estate has been sealed off to visitors since your grandparents left."

The storm raged outside but the stone walls of the dovecote held fast, and they clung to each other, quiet with their own thoughts. The dream flashed before her eyes again. Isabelle running through the gardens, her white nightgown fluttering behind her like a dove in flight. And the birds, so many white doves lying dead at her feet, their hearts ripped out. The image was burned in her mind, and fear exploded inside of her.

"Bastian, make me forget. Just for a while. Please." She tilted her face up to his and kissed his chin, desperate to connect with him and lose herself in him. Even if it could only be temporary. When they kissed, he could help her escape the suffocating sense of fear.

"Jane," he whispered helplessly, and then he took her mouth.

He backed her against the wall and rocked his hips against hers. His erection pressed into her stomach. It wasn't enough. She needed him to be closer, to feel skin to skin. The sharp ache in her womb demanded he be inside her, filling her until they were fused together, wanting nothing more than that simple, primal connection. His lips trailed hot kisses down her neck, and he nipped her shoulder. She clawed at his jacket, and he started to shrug it off when a pale blue light filled the dovecote. The light blossomed, and the temperature around them dropped causing their breaths to emerge as thick white clouds.

"Oh my God!" she gasped, her heart slamming against her ribs, and then it was too late. White light flashed all around them, and then all went dark.

She blinked, trying to see. Pale light started to fade in around the edges, and she recognized where she was. Inside Stormclyffe Hall, in a room on the second floor, overlooking the dovecote and the gardens. Isabelle stood next to her with haunted eyes. She touched Jane's hand and started to speak, her voice barely a whisper at first.

"Jane…Jane you must see… Why can't you see? She's

here. She's still here." Isabelle raised a hand, pointing to the dovecote. Next to it, a spot of blackened earth stretched long enough to cover a body. The roses nearest the earth had withered and died.

"Who's still here?" she asked, eyes locked on that abnormally dark soil.

"She is. The one who pushed me. You know, Jane. I chose you because you would know what happened to me. Blood of my blood, flesh of my flesh, you must stop her. You have to rid my home of her before—" Isabelle spun and faced the door to the room they were in and a bloodcurdling scream tore from her lips.

"Isabelle!" Jane turned to see what scared the other woman, and her heart stopped. There in front of her was a woman in a red cloak, her face decayed as though a flesh-eating disease had ravaged her beautiful features. She reached a clawed hand out toward Jane, and black eyes held red pinpricks which gleamed at their centers.

"You…" The raspy whisper felt like ice picks racking her eardrums. "You will die…as she did. The earl is mine…"

A black wind rose up around them, filling the room until only Isabelle's screams and that awful rasping were mixed with the violent roaring.

"Who are you?" Jane screamed as claws raked her face and hands, drawing blood and scouring bone.

The woman in the red cloak laughed, and it sounded like the cackle of thousand demons from the darkest pits of hell. Jane reached for her necklace, and the second her fingers curled around it, it burned her, but she didn't let it go.

"Jane!" A masculine voice broke through the roaring wind and abruptly the nightmare faded. She was back in the dovecote with Bastian, and her body trembled so hard, her bones felt like they were knocking together.

"Jane, what the bloody hell just happened? You were

having a seizure, and you screamed. God, it was awful, and your face…" Bastian stroked his fingertips over her cheeks. Pain followed his touch.

"What do you mean, my face?" she asked, touching her skin. Raised marks met her fingertips.

"It looks like something clawed your face. But I was holding you the entire time, nothing touched you. The marks don't appear to be bleeding, just welts."

She could barely see his face in the dim light, but she could see enough to tell he was pale, and his brows were knitted together. She couldn't tell him what she'd just seen. It was too insane. Dreams, nightmares, those were normal, excusable products of her imagination. This…this had been something else entirely. She'd feared the other dreams had been evidence of insanity, but this was proof. She wasn't going crazy.

He cupped the sides of her neck with his palms and touched his forehead to hers, their warm breath shared. Gone was the icy chill and the cloudy breaths. Whatever had been here with them a few seconds ago had vanished.

"Jane, love, talk to me. What happened?" The way he said "love" with his British accent, melted her on the inside. She shut her eyes.

"You wouldn't believe me. You'd probably think I was crazy."

"Try me." He kissed her closed eyelids, then the tip of her nose, and finally her lips. "Have a little faith in me, bookworm." He smiled against her mouth, and she couldn't help but smile back.

"You have to stop calling me that," she replied, trying to chastise him, but it came out more teasing than anything else.

"Absolutely not."

"Why?" Her body heated with desire.

"I need to remind myself who you are, that you are off-limits for me. But damned if I can't keep my hands off you, even though I shouldn't want you." He sucked her bottom lip into his mouth.

"I shouldn't want you either," she replied before he distracted her completely. "Mmm…" She moaned in sheer pleasure, the frightening memories of minutes ago fading when he touched her. She was safe with him, well, all except her heart.

"Now," he said between nibbling kisses. "Tell me what happened."

With a shaky sigh, she gave in. "I saw Isabelle. She and I were in the castle looking down at the dovecote, and then this woman attacked us. She looked…horrible. Flesh was decaying and falling off her, and she clawed my face."

He didn't say anything for several seconds. "All right… There was no way you could have made those scratches to yourself. Who was the woman who did this?"

She shrugged. "I'm not sure who. Isabelle just told me to protect her home, and that this woman was still here. She said I was blood of her blood, flesh of her flesh. I don't know what that means. And there was something weird about the dovecote. There was this blackened spot of earth, and all the grass and plants near it had died. Isabelle was pointing at it."

"If you did see Isabelle, then that means the curse—" He brushed a hand over his suddenly pale face as he struggled for words. Outside the storm's ferocity lessened.

"Blood of her blood? That implies kinship, family. Do you know anything of your ancestry?"

"A little. My family has always lived in Charleston on both sides of my parents' lines. I know that one of my ancestors on my mother's side was from England. Joseph Brax. He was the first to come over to America in my mother's family, around 1820 or so."

"Brax?" Bastian tensed.

"Yes." She bit her lip and studied him.

"Jane, Isabelle had a younger brother. Joseph Braxton. He was often called Brax as a nickname according to letters we have from Richard and Isabelle."

What he said took a moment to sink in. "Wait…you're saying that I'm…related to you?" She covered her mouth, horrified.

He gripped her shoulders. "Jane, we're several generations apart, from a distantly connected bloodline. But yes, we're family. You are blood of Isabelle's blood."

For a second Jane just started at him. She and Bastian were related. *Related*. If it hadn't been so many generations apart, she would have been freaked out. But then again, being related was…amazing. She was connected to Isabelle's line.

"Okay, so we're connected a common ancestry."

"Yes," Bastian said. "What else did Isabelle mention? You said something about a dovecote and blackened earth?"

A bone-deep chill burned through her as an awful idea surfaced.

"Bastian, you don't think that…" She gulped, unable for a moment to voice the horrifying thought. "That maybe there's a body buried there?"

He had been stroking her hair, but his hand stilled, and his fingers tightened in the strands.

"What makes you think it's a body?" he asked.

She tensed. "Isabelle said I had to get 'her' out, and I saw this woman with a decaying face and blond hair. She was… horrifying. It seemed like Isabelle was frightened of her and wanted me to get her out of Stormclyffe. How would we know if there's a body there?"

"There's only one way to find out." He gently set her aside and headed for the dovecote's door.

The storm had melted into a heavy rain. He went outside and disappeared around the side of the building, soon returning to the doorway with an ancient shovel in his hand. She drank in the sight of him with his rain-slicked, golden hair. He glanced about on the ground and then looked back at her.

"Where did you see the spot?" he asked.

She moved into the doorway and pointed at the particular area she remembered all too vividly from the dream. With a heavy nod, he slammed the shovel's tip deep into the earth and pressed his foot on the metal, using his weight to plunge it even deeper. Rain sluiced over his body and the cold earth as he dug. For the next hour, she watched in fear and silence as he continued to dig his shovel into the soil. When the hole was three feet deep and three feet long, he suddenly dropped the shovel and stumbled back a step with a guttural shout.

"What is it?" She crept out of the building and placed her hands on his shoulder.

He pointed toward the hole. Apprehension dug its venom-tipped nails into her spine as she crept to the edge and peered down. She clamped a hand over her mouth to stifle her scream.

Pale bones. Human remains jutted out of the blackened soil. Remnants of a red velvet cloak tangled with the dirt and white fragments.

"There are bones in my gardens," he declared slowly. "Bones. Christ, what the bloody hell am I supposed to do? Call the police?"

She gripped his arm hard as she felt something foreign move through her, whispering to her. *"Destroy them. Cast them into the sea. She must not stay here any longer."*

"We have to get rid of them. Throw them over the cliff," she urged.

"What?" He glanced down at her, startled. "No, Jane, we have to call the police." He grasped her shoulders and shook her.

She cast the strange compulsion aside, ignoring the need

to obey command to destroy the bones.

"You're right. Of course, you're right. They'll need to process the scene." She knew from the look of the cloak that the body wasn't from this century.

"Come on." He took her hand, lacing their fingers together and leading her away from the shallow grave.

• • •

Bastian was worried, more than he cared to admit. Jane was shaking so violently that her teeth were chattering, and he feared she might get ill if she stayed outside any longer. He would have the cook make her hot soup, and then he'd get into bed and warm her up, with his body if he was lucky.

Guilt settled like stones upon his chest. He'd brought her out here, not knowing what would happen. She was sensitive to the castle and its history. He hadn't realized just how deep that sensitivity ran. Perhaps it was her genetic connection to Isabelle, but he couldn't be sure. More important though, he couldn't deny that what she was seeing and experiencing involved a history she would know nothing about. His family kept their secrets well, and the fact that she was finding out things even he didn't know meant something was going on. He didn't want to label it as paranormal or supernatural. He wasn't ready to do that yet. But Jane had witnessed a vision that led to him digging up a body.

Protecting Jane was paramount. The blank look on her face as her voice turned cold and hard as she demanded he get rid of the bones had chilled the blood in his veins. In that moment, he was reminded of his grandmother and her strange behavior in connection to Stormclyffe. His mother, too, had always behaved oddly whenever he mentioned the Hall. He glanced over his shoulder back at the hole near the dovecote and the bones.

Whose remains were they? And how had they ended up there? What did they have to do with Isabelle?

Randolph stood at the top of the stone steps near the south door, facing the gardens. A large black umbrella curved over his head like bat wings. When he noticed them, he jogged out to meet them, handing Bastian the umbrella to shield him and Jane.

"Thank you, Randolph." He nodded at his butler and wrapped an arm around Jane's shoulders as he took her inside.

"You're welcome, my lord. Is there anything else you need?" The older man shrugged out of his coat and reached for theirs.

"Yes, please phone the police and tell them to come at once. We've found human remains on the property, old ones."

Randolph stilled, his gray brows lowering over his dark eyes. "Remains?"

Bastian pressed a kiss to Jane's forehead, drawing strength from her closeness before he answered.

"They are by the dovecote."

"How did you find them?"

It was Jane who replied to Randolph this time, and Bastian wished she hadn't. "I saw it in a vision."

Bastian's body absorbed the shudder that racked her, as he stroked her hair back from her face. She was so damned strong, but still, she roused every protective instinct inside him and drew out every gentle and sweet need in him to care for her and reassure her. He'd never felt this way with any woman he'd been with in the past. Sex was all he'd ever sought. He wondered if some part of his subconscious avoided romantic entanglements that might put any woman he started to care about in danger from his family's tragic curse. But Jane was proving impossible to avoid.

She was the exception to every rule he'd made in his life. She was a snag in the grand design, a twist of unexpected thread in the dull tapestry destiny was weaving. It was all coming undone, and the loose threads were spiraling around him in tantalizing patterns and colors. She was saving him from the slow slip down a dark, lonely path. She dragged him back, forced him to live, breath after painful breath, until he started to become the man his father would have been proud of.

"My lord, before you call the police. I must speak with you." Randolph's eyes were wide and sorrowful. "Both of you."

Bastian gave a curt nod. "Let's go to the Egyptian room. The fire should be lit, and it's a good place to talk."

Randolph led the way through the halls and they passed through the room of marble statues. More than once, Bastian's skin crawled, and he could have sworn that some of the heads of the marble men and women turned his way as he passed by.

The Egyptian room was one of his favorites. All of the furniture had lionlike paws on the legs and several of the couches had sphinx bodies holding up the armrests. Gilded palm fronds extended up from the base of the walls and a rich red paint covered the top part of the entire room and turned purple toward the ceiling, making it feel as though one were actually in Egypt watching the sun set over the banks of the Nile. The ceiling itself was dark blue with dozens of constellations made from diamonds embedded in the plaster. They glittered sharp and clear as any stars in the night sky.

He took a seat on one of the couches, pulling Jane down beside him while keeping his arm firmly around her shoulders. Randolph paced over to the fire, peering into the flames.

"I know you do not believe in spirits, my lord, but I must speak of them tonight." He turned to face them. Outside, twilight was creeping along the horizon, her mauve tendrils slithering through the clouds as she slowly devoured the day.

Randolph had never spoke of ghosts, never seemed to

give credence to the ghost stories told by the townspeople. So to hear him even say the word was…chilling.

"Many years ago, when I was a young man, I spent my first summer here as a lad working for your grandfather. He was a good man. When he fell in love with your grandmother though…ahh how he loved her," Randolph paused. "That was when the trouble began. She started having nightmares, ones that made her scream."

Jane flinched and burrowed closer to Bastian. "Like me."

"Shh…it's all right," he murmured in her ear.

"She began to walk in her sleep, roaming the halls, talking of shadows and a woman in red. An evil woman who we had to get out of the house. And then…Nessy, your grandmother's, maid died. The police ruled it as a suicide, but I knew her; she was a friend. She would never have killed herself." His voice broke a little. "Rumors flew around town blaming your grandfather. But none of it was true. That…that evil thing was what killed her." Randolph uttered the last few words so harshly that both Bastian and Jane clutched each other tight.

"What evil thing?" Jane asked, although she feared she knew the answer.

The butler smoothed a hand over his balding head. "A ghost, a spirit, a demonic presence? Whatever it is that dwells in this house, it is jealous. Any woman who dares to love a man of Carlisle blood has met a bloody end. It was the reason your grandfather took your grandmother and fled this place. He saved her." Randolph sank down onto the couch opposite them, his eyes deeply focused on something long years past. "I thought the cycle was broken, but your father…came back. And it took him like it did all of the others who've tried to live happy lives. I didn't want you to come here either, but you were so stubborn, so drawn to this place." He smiled. "Like father, like son. Now that evil has its hooks in Miss Seyton. She's in danger, my lord. You must acknowledge that, even if you choose not to believe in spirits." He stood again, as though any period of immobility disturbed him.

"Whatever you have uncovered by the dovecote, it must be removed. Have the police take it away tonight if possible. We might rid ourselves of the evil at last." He walked to the door and looked back. "I will have Mrs. Beechum make soup for you, and I will call for you when it's ready."

Bastian's throat was so tight he could barely breathe. The butler was always taking care of him, just as he cared for the two previous earls of Stormclyffe, and it had cost him nearly as much as it had cost Bastian.

"Thank you, Randolph." He hoped the elderly man would know his words went beyond a simple thanks.

"It is my duty." Randolph bowed and disappeared.

"Do you believe me now?" Jane's voice was quiet and she looked up at him, her lovely lashes framing those eyes he adored.

"Against every logical bone in my body, I'm starting to." He slid his hand in his pocket, retrieved his phone. It was time to put an end to the vicious cycle that was hurting his family and those he cared about.

A female operator answered the phone. "999, what's your emergency?"

He cleared his throat. "I need to report a body."

Chapter Eleven

The police arrived half an hour later, swarming Stormclyffe as they studied the bones by the dovecote. From the safety of a window overlooking the gardens, Jane watched the activity. An anthropologist, who'd come upon Bastian's request, finished photographing and mapping the site. The bones appeared to be very old.

The authorities removed the remains, packed them into a coroner's vehicle, and drove off after midnight. A breath of relief escaped her lips as she watched the last van's taillights fade into the darkness. She should have felt better now that the body was gone, but she didn't. Had she expected the stones around her to expel a sigh of relief when the source of evil had been removed? Probably. The feel of a dark taint still clouded her senses, as though the bones had leached evil into the soil and air.

Whatever she and Bastian were caught up in might not be over yet. The air around her seemed charged like minutes before a storm was about to break or on the eve of battle, when warriors put on their polished armor, slid broadswords in their sheaths, and prayed to their gods for victory in hushed voices as dawn grew upon the horizon.

"If only we knew what we are facing," she murmured and turned away from the window. She was back in the Egyptian room. It was fast becoming one of her favorite places. She was comforted by the distant gazes of the sphinxes. The palm fronds seemed to almost ripple with the gentle rustle of real plants. If she closed her eyes, the room would carry her away, like a boat upon the waters of the Nile.

With a little shake, she dragged herself back to the present. Every room in the castle had this effect on her. Each whispered and teased her with visions of lives lived and days long past.

It was time to open the floodgates. Let the muses from other eras whisper their truths. She would unravel the mystery and save Stormclyffe from the evil that haunted its rightful heirs. She had to do it; no one else could. She felt it deep in her bones. Bastian finally believed her, and would be by her side.

She settled into one of the couches by the fire and kicked her boots off. Something dug into her spine, and she reached behind her. Her fingers slid over smooth leather, and she pulled out a book.

Richard's journal. How had it gotten here? She knew for a fact that she'd left it in her bag upstairs. A sudden gale tore through the fireplace, sending the flames lashing out like vengeful fire demons, causing her to flinch. The pages of the journal fluttered open, the first line catching her attention.

October 31st, 1811

I am happy. No man has ever been as lucky as I have been. I love my wife. Wife. What a wondrous word. She is everything to me. Today, of all glorious days since I've met her, is perhaps the best. Our child, Edward, was born this afternoon. Never had an infant cried so loud, and I laughed with delight at the sound. Isabelle looked up at me, sweat beaded upon her brow, her body limp with exhaustion from bringing our son into the world. All I saw was how beautiful she was, how in awe I was of her for doing something I could never do. She made our lives complete, more complete than I knew we could be. I cradled our babe and sat next to her in bed, allowing her a moment to sleep, knowing the baby and I were within her reach.

I am a father! There was nothing more humbling and more wonderful than helping to bring a life into the world. I was struck with pride and yet feel unworthy of the gift of this little boy. He stirred and cooed softly like a new dove from a nest, and my heart overflowed with love. I counted his fingers, marveling at the tiny perfections, and I cradled his head with my hand, stroking the fine dark hair that was so like his mother's. I hoped he will grow up to look like her and possess that same dark alluring beauty. The young ladies in the village will have their hearts broken when the day comes for him to choose his wife. The thought makes me smile. Someday my son will marry and know the happiness I have found with his mother.

A knock disturbed my peaceful thoughts. My butler peered into the room, eyes dark with concern.

"What is it?"

"My lord, you must come at once. We have a situation at the dovecote."

I would have ignored the request but Shrewsbury's tone warned me that it was important. I placed my son in his new cradle, then followed my butler out to the gardens.

Several of the groundskeepers were waiting near the dovecote, faces solemn. At their feet were dozens of little white shapes. As I drew closer, I realized they were doves. Dead doves. Streaks of crimson marred the snowy perfection of their breasts. My soul cried out at the loss of their lives.

"What has happened to them?" I demanded.

"Something ripped their hearts out. Everyone one of them

is dead, save for this one." One of the older groundskeepers, Samuel Allen, held out his weathered hands and placed a small young dove into my palms.

I cupped my hands delicately around the bird, and it cooed softly and thrashed a little against my restrictive hold.

"That one was hiding at the top." Samuel pointed to the cupola. "Whoever did this missed it."

"Who?" I asked, something dark and angry digging into my spine as I thought of what man would have done this to innocent creatures.

"A man must have done this." Samuel scrubbed blood off his hands, leaving dark tracts on his woolen pants. "No animal would have left the bodies. Beasts eat what they kill."

One of the younger men shifted restless. "T'was witchcraft," he muttered.

My gaze flicked to his. "Witchcraft?" I held up the dove and stared into his black eyes. He bobbed his head, as though eyeing me with equal scrutiny.

"Hearts of innocent creatures," the man elaborated. "A witch would use them in spells, according to me mum." He trailed off, cheeks turning a ruddy red.

"Why my doves?" I studied the dovecote. It had been built for Isabelle, one of my wedding gifts to her.

"Perhaps someone wishes to do you ill." Samuel's rough rumble sent a shudder through me.

"I do not know anyone who wished to do me harm." Even as I spoke the words, I felt as though I was forgetting something. That forgotten piece nagged at the back of my mind, yet I could not seem to catch the last thought and drag it into the light.

I returned the surviving dove to Samuel's care and instructed him to care for it. The need to be back with Isabelle and my son was too strong to be ignored. I had to hold them both in my arms and reassure myself they were safe. If someone wished to do me ill, then they were in grave danger.

• • •

"Jane." Bastian's voice was a low, gentle whisper in her ear.

She stirred, and her lashes fluttered up.

"Was I asleep?" she murmured. She was reclined on the couch, and Bastian was sitting on the edge, one hand braced on the back of the couch by her head as he leaned over. Worried lines marred his brow.

"Yes, I just came to fetch you. It's nearly two in the morning. You must be tired. Let me take you to your room." He brushed stray tendrils of her hair back and stroked her cheek with his the back of his knuckles. The intimate touch warmed her inside, and she leaned into the caress before she caught herself. He made it so easy to forget that things between them wouldn't work out. Still, she kept kissing him, getting closer and closer to him, when she knew she shouldn't.

"Are the police gone?" she asked.

Bastian's gaze strayed to the fire, weariness carving age in his youthful face.

"Yes. The last detective just left. I convinced them they didn't need to see you. The anthropologist confirmed the age of the bones and there's no suspicion of foul play by anyone alive. They will continue their examination of the bones to determine the cause of death. The good news is they won't have to come back, and the bones will stay away from us and Stormclyffe."

She sat up, bringing herself closer to him. "Thank goodness." The tension coiled tight in her was finally released and exhaustion turned her limbs to lead. Her mouth stretched with a yawn, which made him smile.

"I think I need to get you into bed." After his words sank in they both stared at each other before he chuckled, his cheeks turning red. He hastily corrected himself. "Let me take you to *your* bed, so you can sleep."

"Thanks." She let him help her up, trying not to dwell on the idea of him sharing her bed again. Last night had been good, too good. God knows how good it would be if they ever had sex. The thought had her body heating and her face flushing. Making love with Bastian would break her into a thousand pieces and remake her. She doubted she'd survive the pleasure of it.

They were close to the door when she remembered Richard's journal.

"Wait! I have to get the diary." She turned back but the couch was empty. There was no sign of the diary.

"Jane?"

She spun to face him, her heart beating rapidly. "Bastian, I was reading the journal. There was an entry about the murdered doves. My vision was right! The diary was right here." She ran her fingers over the couch, but no journal was lodged beneath the cushions.

"You're sure it was here?" Bastian's tone was tinged with skepticism.

"Yes. I swear." She frowned at him, annoyed that he wouldn't believe her.

He leaned against the doorjamb. "That little book has the strangest propensity to wander off and turn up in the most unusual places. I'm sure it will show up again when it wishes to be found." His lips twitched.

"It's not funny. It was here. You have to believe me."

He curled an arm around her waist and brushed a kiss against her temple. "I do, Jane. We'll find it in the morning."

He walked her to her room and left her there at the threshold.

"You aren't staying with me?" Her question came out a whisper and she hated how weak she sounded.

With a quick shake of his head he replied. "No. I can't. Don't you see, Jane? I allowed myself to get close to you, to entertain a hope that we might be something more, and you suffered a vision in the dovecote that led to a body in my garden."

"I had the visions long before I met you," she reminded him softly, hurt that he would use that against her. Just like Tim had.

"I know, but if I start to believe you, then I have to believe our getting close could lead to more things, Jane. Dangerous things. I don't want you at any more risk than you have to be. I wanted…" He trailed off, cleared his throat. "What I want is not what I can have right now, which means I will bid you good night." He spun on his heel and left.

She wanted to call him back, ask him to stay with her, but she was already falling too far for him. Instead, she watched him stride down the hall, his body moving with the sleek grace of a panther, and it made her ache deep inside. Another cold night alone was all she had to look forward to, that and the nightmares that would surely come.

• • •

Research proved a fruitless endeavor the day after the body had been discovered. Jane couldn't think clearly. After three hours of staring at the record books in front of her she hadn't read a thing. With a sigh, she shoved her chair back. Frustration made her skin prickle with irritation. The only thing she wanted to read was the journal.

It was missing. She and Bastian had sifted through the books and papers in every single room they could think of. Yet there was no sign of it. The one piece of history that held the clues to her research and the mystery of Isabelle's death had vanished. Jane needed a break. There wouldn't be any more productivity, not with the mood she was in.

"*Jane.*" Bastian's voice made her look up from her notes.

There was no one there. Had she imagined it? Surely that was it. She was missing him and her brain had supplied his voice. She had been avoiding him most of the day since she was mortified after last night's rejection.

As thoughts of him started to cloud her mind, she cocked her head to the side to study the most peculiar sight. A silvery nimbus-like shape near the doorway of the library caught her attention. The shock of seeing it froze her in place.

"Jane…" The voice this time wasn't Bastian's, but it was a man's voice. Her skin rippled with goose bumps. *"Come to me, Jane."* The hypnotic pull of his voice drew her to her feet like a marionette on strings. She drifted toward the door, completely out of control, her sense of awareness of this time and place slipping away as another time took hold of her. Shadows stretched across the floor, touching her feet, coiling up around her legs like serpents. Her mouth parted, a scream almost escaping her lips before she was silenced.

Her nightgown whipped about her ankles like the panicked flapping of a dying bird. There wasn't time. She had to escape before the evil claimed her. Richard was asleep in bed, their baby son in his crib next to the bed. It was all lost to her. She had to get out, get out before she died. The great oak door crashed open as she threw her body against it. Rain lashed her body as she fled into the night and the storm. Rocks cut her feet, and yet she kept running. Run! Run! *the voice in her head screeched, shrilling like a banshee crying out her doom.*

She reached the cliffs and froze, her toes digging into the rocky ledge, her arms cartwheeling as she tried to keep from falling off the cliff. Once her balance was regained, she forced herself back a step to safety.

"You little whore!" A feminine shriek burst her eardrums, and someone's hands dug into her back, shoving her.

Lightning streaked across the sky, and she fell.

Chapter Twelve

"My lord!" Randolph appeared in the doorway of Bastian's study, gasping and red-faced. One of his hands was clutching his chest.

"What?" Bastian jumped to his feet in an instant and ran to meet his butler.

"It's Miss Seyton. She's headed for the north tower. I tried to stop her, but she was too strong. She was muttering about shadows."

The north tower? What was Jane doing? She could get hurt up there. The stairs were mostly rotted wood that hadn't been replaced or repaired in a century. He'd kept it locked up until last week to keep any workmen from getting hurt.

"Damn!" he bellowed and took off running, leaving Randolph behind.

She was talking about shadows? His grandmother's warning echoed in his head. *"Beware the shadows…"* His boots slapped the stone stairs as he reached the doorway to the north tower. It was wide open, the weathered wood covered in cobwebs on one side as he sprinted past. Gripping the edges of the narrow stone wall, he prayed the creaking steps wouldn't collapse beneath him.

"Jane!"

Two more flights. He couldn't get his feet to move fast enough. When he passed through the doorway at the top of the stairs, he slid to a halt.

She was a few feet away, standing between the gray stone turrets on the ledge. Her arms were open and her head tilted back. Her arms suddenly dropped to her sides, and his breath hitched when she looked over her shoulder at him.

"Jane…get down from the ledge." He tried to keep his voice smooth and calm. "*Please*." He crept toward her, hoping it wouldn't catch her off guard and make her fall. As he got closer, his heart pounded in his chest as he saw her eyes.

They were red and glowing like the flames of a distant fire.

"She's coming." Jane's voice seemed merged with another woman's voice.

"Who?" He was so close, if she just stepped off the ledge toward him, he could catch her.

"The heart of evil." That same early eerie, dual voice rippled over his skin with an almost tangible touch. She started to lean away from him when the wind rose up enough to push her off the ledge. He shouted and dove for her.

His fingers dug into her sweater, snagging her just in time. With a violent tug, he brought her flying back into him. They stumbled, and he grunted as they slammed hard into the floor. She was limp in his arms, her eyes closed and breathing shallow. For a few precious seconds, he fought to regain his breath. He cupped her face and lifted it up so he could see her. She blinked a few times, her eyes a little glassy.

"Are you all right, Jane?" He held her tight, afraid to lose her after what he'd just witnessed. She had nearly fallen to her death. The significance of that wasn't lost on him. Little tremors shook him, and he hoped she couldn't feel his hands shaking.

"Bastian, why are we on the roof?" She glanced about, eyes wide, lips trembling.

"You came up here on your own. Randolph saw you and said you were muttering about shadows. He came and got me straightaway. I got here just in time to catch you before you fell."

Before Jane could respond, Randolph appeared in the open stairwell doorway.

"My lord!" His wheezing breaths announced he'd run the entire way.

"She's fine. I've got her."

The old butler sagged with relief. "Thank heavens."

"Bastian, I was dreaming, I think. I was Isabelle, and I was fleeing the castle and heading toward the cliffs." She licked her lips nervously. "Something was urging me to run. I didn't have any control." The last few words that left her mouth wavered as she fought off emotions.

"Easy love, it's over now." He wanted to ease her fears and never feel her heart beating so frantically against his again, unless it was from wild lovemaking.

"Is it really? What if this keeps happening until I eventually jump?"

Bastian shook his head. "I won't let that happen. If I have to keep you with me every second of the day to protect you, I will." His voice was a low growl. He prayed that she would believe him.

"You can't promise that," she argued.

"I can." He lifted her away from him so he could sit up.

"But you said you had to stay away from me to keep me safe."

He exhaled a slow breath. "Apparently I was wrong. You're a target whether I'm near you or not. I can't afford to let anything happen to you. You should leave now. Go back home to Charleston and never look back." He meant it. Part of him wanted to have an excuse to be near her but he hated that the cost was her life being in danger, more so than he'd ever imagined. It wasn't just the fear of an accident like his father's death. There was more to this, something far more sinister and otherworldly. How could he even begin to protect her against something like that?

Her fear-tinged stare roamed over the turrets, then back to Bastian. "I'm not leaving. I think Isabelle was murdered. Something was chasing and pushed her off the cliff. We have to find out what, or who, it was."

"Then we'll need to find Richard's journal." If there was an answer that hadn't been erased by the passage of time, that journal might hold the key to the mystery. He caught Jane's hands and they both stood.

"Why don't you both rest before dinner?" Randolph suggested.

After the terror of seeing Jane almost die, Bastian had to admit, rest seemed like a good idea. His own heart was still pounding violently.

The three of them began the long descent from the north tower. When they arrived at Jane's room, she hesitated, her gaze shifting as she studied the room as though she expected to be attacked.

"I'm right across the hall if you need me. I'll watch over you and wake you when it's time for dinner."

She looked so uneasy that it made an invisible fist crush his heart. He curled his hands around her waist and brought her close for a lingering, comforting kiss.

"I'll be here."

"Thank you," she murmured and drew back. She slid into her room and closed the door.

Bastian remained there a few minutes longer, debating

whether he should stay with her or return to his own room. Surely she would be fine, she was only a few feet away if she needed him. He turned his back on her and entered his room.

He didn't jump this time when he saw Richard's journal lying open on his bed. He didn't dwell on it or how it got there. There was little point in questioning the diary's ability to appear and disappear at will. Instead, he focused on the answers he and Jane needed. If Isabelle had been murdered, it changed everything.

There was no date at the top of the journal, and it was much later than the other entries Richard had written.

It began with nightmares. For the last three nights, Isabelle has woken me and Edward with her guttural screams. Each time I did my best to comfort her, but I know it is not enough. Her eyes are haunted and ringed with purple bruises from lack of sleep. She is terrified to close her eyes. Before the screaming starts, she whispers about shadows and "that creature" which she cannot cast out. After each incident, I questioned her, but she cannot recall what she's dreamed.

Samuel, my old gardener has taken to following her about whenever she goes out on the grounds. I thanked him. He will watch over her when I cannot. Isabelle's condition frightens me. There is nothing so terrifying in the world than to watch an invisible monster attack someone you love. How do I slay her dragon if I cannot see it? I am afraid she is close to breaking…

. . .

The lines on the page scrawled off as though the writer had been interrupted. Bastian fingered the pages of the journal, wondering what had made Richard stop writing. One thing was clear.

The past was repeating itself. Whatever dark force that held Stormclyffe in thrall had fixated on Jane like it had

Isabelle. Richard's words carved themselves into his chest.

How do I slay her dragon if I cannot see it?

What was the dragon? A mental condition created by stress and influenced by Isabelle's own madness, or was the answer something far more sinister and otherworldly? He didn't want to acknowledge that, but too much had happened for him to deny something beyond his understanding was happening in his home. Seeing Jane standing on the edge of the turrets had forced him to acknowledge that something dark lived within his home and wanted to hurt him and those he cared about.

His phone buzzed in his pocket, and he was oddly relieved to see his mother's number. He hadn't spoken to her in weeks.

"Bastian?" His mother's voice came through the phone clearly.

"Mother, how are you?" he asked.

"Fine, fine. How are the renovations coming?" Her question was ordinary, but he detected a strain to her tone he hadn't heard before.

"Mother, what is it?" The fine hairs on the back of his neck lifted from an invisible wind.

"I was taking a nap this afternoon and had a most peculiar dream. There was a woman with dark hair. You were holding her close and kissing her."

Normally he would have blanched at his mother dreaming of him in a romantic setting with a woman, but something about her voice still unsettled him.

"What else did you dream about?"

His mother's soft sigh made his chest tighten. "She's real isn't she? The woman? You care about her." That last part wasn't a question.

"I…do. Against all rationality, I care about her." Admitting it aloud felt strangely freeing and yet frightening. He couldn't take what he said back.

"Be careful, sweetheart."

"What is it?" he prompted.

"I saw this woman wreathed in darkness and consumed by shadows. She's in danger, Bastian. Watch over her. You need to get yourself and her away from that awful place." His mother's warning was an echo of his own instincts, but they were so close to solving the mystery of the place.

He had to stay. The compulsion to be at Stormclyffe overrode logic. He had to restore the castle, fix it. They had to mend what once was broken. There would be no rest, no safety until it was done. He knew this to be true deep within his bones. Neither he nor Jane could back out now, not until they saw this through.

"I will keep her safe, Mother." A flicker of nerves made him hesitate briefly. "Christmas is a few months away, I would like for you to meet her."

His mother was silent a long moment. "How long have you known her?"

This time Bastian laughed. "A handful of days." How could he explain it? The magnetic pull, the sense that he'd always known her. From the moment she'd turned around in the red drawing room with Isabelle's portrait behind her, he'd been struck by that startling likeness. Seeing her seemed to have roused him from a hundred years of enchanted sleep.

"Your father asked me to marry him three minutes after he met me." His mother's words cut into his thoughts.

"What? I didn't know that." Bastian smiled.

"The only reason I said yes was because of how he danced. He didn't say a word, just took me in his arms, and we danced. When the music was over, he got down on one knee in front of everyone and proposed. He said he would never find a partner as perfect as me, so he stopped looking."

He put a hand over his heart as his chest tightened. It never ceased to amaze him that grief which had long since been buried could resurface after just one beautiful memory of a lost loved one.

"If this Jane is your perfect partner, time stops. You don't have to think past that."

He didn't respond but instead said, "I'll see you at Christmas." Perfect partner? They'd danced around each other, and the chemistry was hot enough to burn, but he sensed she craved more, even as she feared it. Just like he did.

"I love you, dear. Please be careful. I can't lose you, too." The quiet despair in her tone made his eyes burn.

"You won't, Mother. This is my home. I am not going to let shadows of the past chase me away."

· · ·

Jane couldn't sleep. Instead she sprawled on the bed, her laptop up and running as she researched ghosts. There were thousands of sites dedicated to hauntings and paranormal activity. Several spiritualists suggested that ghosts who suffered tragic events would repeat the event over and over again, like a broken record. Supposedly, if someone could get the spirit to break the cycle, then the spirit would be able to move on.

She stared into the distance, thinking back to when she had seen Isabelle on the cliffs and how she had been pulled off the ledge by thorny, black roots. The gardener had mentioned that she haunted the cliffs and been seen there many times. Maybe she reenacted her death over and over again, and this was the cycle Jane needed to break.

Closing her eyes, she let the memory of the cliffs come back. She had been Isabelle and felt what Isabelle had felt. The terror and despair and the crashing blackness on the rocks below. And then she'd woken up and found that she'd nearly jumped off the north tower.

A shiver slid along her spine. She could have died. *Would* have died if Bastian hadn't been there to save her…

A rapping sound on her door dragged her back from the darkness of her thoughts.

Bastian's voice was quiet, gentle, on the other side of Jane's door. "Are you ready for dinner?"

"Hang on," she called out and dashed to the bathroom.

With a quick check in the mirror to make sure her jeans and sweater looked good, she slid her feet into her ballet flats and took a deep breath.

She opened the door. "Ready."

He leaned lazily against the wall next to her room, one shoulder propping him up, legs crossed at the ankles. He straightened, pulled back the sleeve of his black sweater and examined his Cartier wristwatch.

"We have time for dinner and the ballroom." His lips quirking into a ghost of a smile.

"Ballroom?" she asked. Was he planning to take her into town tonight for dancing? The idea had a fair amount of appeal, but she wasn't the best dancer. Slow dancing was the extent of her talents.

He picked up on her nervousness. "Don't tell me you don't want to see it. We missed it on your official tour. I thought all Americans *loved* their tours."

She groaned and joined him in the hall. "You'll never let me live this down, will you?"

He had the audacity to flash a cheeky grin. "We Brits have long memories. To me, you're still a colonist."

"Jesus, at this rate, we might reach independence from you people when I'm dead."

"Perhaps, if you're lucky." He slid an arm around her waist in a gesture so casual that it felt like he'd done it for years. His fingers curled possessively, and she warmed inside at the intimacy it created. It was almost like he was flirting with her…but surely not. Even though he said he believed her about her dreams now, men like Bastian and women like her never got together. A girl could dream though…

I should pull away. Can't let him get to me, but he's so damned sexy and sweet. The barriers against her heart were like splinters in stone, and the desire to be with him flowed easily like water through the fractures he'd created. He was breaking into her heart, and she was having trouble keeping him out.

He even pulled her chair back for her when they arrived at the dining room. Randolph appeared, accompanied by a plump woman in a flour-covered apron—probably the cook, Mrs. Beechum, who brought their dinner and left.

"Where are they going?" Jane asked after Randolph and the cook disappeared out a small side door.

Bastian sipped his Chianti before replying. "Probably back to Weymouth tonight. He has a few things he wishes to do in town and will return tomorrow. I have been running this place on a skeleton crew for the last couple of months until things settle down. A lot of the workers weren't comfortable with all of the accidents and setbacks on the renovations. Most of them only agreed to work during the day and return to the town before nightfall."

There was no need to clarify what "things" he meant. Ghosts.

"You mean it's just you and me? Alone?" She gulped down her wine.

He chuckled, a playful and wicked gleam in his eyes. "Frightened of being alone with me, Jane? Afraid I'll spread you out on this table and feast on you, that I'll ravish you senseless?" His words came out a silken promise of things to come.

The heat in his eyes reminded her of chocolate, and she was sucked into the image he painted. Her lying on the table, dishes broken on the ground from where he had shoved them away to get to her. His hands ripping at her clothes, desperate to taste her bare flesh…

Wetness pooled between her legs, and she clenched her thighs together, thankful he couldn't see through the table. She bit her bottom lip and looked away, desperate to hide the desire in her eyes. If he ever found out how much she wanted him, wanted what his kisses promised, she would be in trouble.

"Jane, I was only teasing." He pushed back his chair and stood.

"I'm fine, really. I think I'm just on edge, that's all."

She took a bite of her roasted chicken.

He walked over to her and placed his hands on her shoulders. She looked over her shoulder, surprised at how vulnerable she felt in that moment.

Yet there was something impossibly arousing to have him behind her when she was defenseless. He dug his long, elegant fingers into her muscles, rubbing the tension away. A moan slipped from her, and her head fell back against the chair.

He looked down at her, his gaze filled with a scorching heat that burned her from the inside. She'd never thought she could drown in a man's eyes, but staring up at him, she finally understood. His black pupils dilated rapidly, absorbing her as they absorbed the light in the room. Nothing existed outside of him, nothing mattered beyond the promise of dark delights and carnal pleasures that were reflected in his predatory stare. She surrendered to that gaze, to him.

He continued to massage her, all of that strength and power he possessed targeted at making her relax. She blinked. Thoughts like that sure could go straight to a girl's head, make her want to whimper, beg, and surrender to anything he might demand. She'd never been the submissive type, but a man who could dominate her sensually set her blood on fire.

"Why the blush?" he asked, his voice amused. His hand settled on her throat, his fingers curling around it. He didn't squeeze, but the grip was possessive. She got even wetter, her thighs, shaking from how tight they were smashed together.

"It's a little warm in here." Her tongue was thick as molasses. She was having trouble concentrating on anything besides the memory of his full lips, how they kissed with such natural ease. How good it felt to be under his control, consumed by his need for her.

"Finish your dinner. You'll feel better with a full stomach." He trailed his fingertips along the nape of her neck, toying with her hair, pulling it to one side so he could caress the knotted muscles on either side of her neck before he returned to his seat.

She ate rapidly, not really hungry, thankful for the distraction. Anything to get her mind off Bastian and the new power he seemed to have over her.

He cleaned his plate first and then sat back, watching her.

"What is the one thing you miss most about your home?" he asked.

She set her fork down and contemplated that. The answer came fairly easily.

"When I was ten, my dad took us out on his sailboat on the ocean. He had this old brass bell. That morning fog drifted across the lake, and my dad rang the bell to warn other boats we were nearby. I loved the sound of that bell. When my father sold that boat, he removed the bell, made a wind chime out of it, and hung it on a window outside my room." Before she even realized it, she was smiling, but her chest was tight as she realized how much she missed home and that sound.

She raised her gaze to his face. "There's nothing more wonderful than hearing the clanging early in the morning as a breeze moves through the trees." A blush heated her face as she realized she was picturing him in bed next to her, listening to the bell chime, while their bodies were wrapped around each other.

To distract herself, she turned the question back to him. "What about you? Do you miss something back in London?"

He played with the stem of his wineglass, watching the way the candlelight glinted off the crystal. "I miss…" He hesitated, cleared his throat and then continued. "I miss feeling like I have a place of my own. London was never my home, even though it's the only place I've ever known. This," he gestured to the beautiful dining room around them, which was adorned with portraits of his ancestors, "this is my home. I feel it in my blood and in my bones. I belong here, and nothing will make me leave. That's why I have to restore this place. I will not let anything take my home away from me."

She heard the silent vow behind that. Ghosts or no ghosts, he wouldn't abandon Stormclyffe to them. It was his home, and he was going to fight for it.

Neither of them spoke after that, and she hastily finished her dinner. He got up first and was at her side, hand outstretched.

"Come with me."

Chapter Thirteen

Bastian held out his hand, hoping Jane would come with him. It made no sense that a woman he'd met only a few days ago seemed suddenly so important. But a stirring deep inside the core of him whispered.

Take her. Protect her. Mine.

After all the women he'd been with, to not merely crave Jane, but want to possess her on some elemental, primal level confounded him. He needed her almost as much as he needed air to breathe. Every rational thought reminded him to keep away, that staying distant would protect her, but it was harder and harder to fight that.

After his father died, he'd believed little else mattered beyond finishing what his father had started. Stormclyffe's restoration was to be a tribute to him and all of the Carlisles who'd come before, haunted by years of tragedy and superstition. Now he realized it was so much more than that. Bringing this place back to life wasn't about creating a tribute but defending what was rightfully his. His father had risked his life coming back because restoring the hall had meant that much to him, and Bastian understood that. Hated it that it had taken his father from him, but the same deep need to fix the castle was within him, too. At any cost.

Slowly Jane put her palm in his. He relished the blossom of rose in her cheeks as her gray eyes flitted to his face, then away and back again.

He led her out of the dining room, down the hall, and into the castle's large ballroom. He'd purposely not taken her there, so he could surprise her, and the wait had been worth it. The ballroom had been renovated in the 1920s, with stained glass windows, crystal chandeliers, and wood floors.

"Oh! The ballroom!" She sighed dreamily. "Did you know that during World War II they housed wounded soldiers here?"

His lips twitched. She may have originally been an intruder bent on prying into his past, but now he understood her interest for what it was. She loved this place as much as he did.

She grasped his hands, delight shining in her eyes. "Dance with me!"

Bastian attempted to step back, shaking his head. "I don't really dance."

With a nibble on her bottom lip, she tugged on his hands. "Just one song. Please."

Sighing, he surrendered and left her in the middle of the room and to walk over to the newly installed entertainment bar off to the side.

He'd had a group of technicians install a sound system in case he wanted to connect an mp3 player into the new speaker system that circled the room. He pulled his phone out of his pocket, scrolled to a playlist, and found a good song before he popped the audio jack in and hit play.

She had her back to him when a musician started to sing "Ain't No Sunshine."

The staccato *bump bump* of the bass and the infusion of orchestra strings filled the air, enveloping them. The music's invisible strings seemed to coil around them as she spun to face him. Her lips formed a little "O" of surprise, her eyes bright with pleasure. He grinned.

She was beautiful. Stunning.

He could see a future with her, and it scared him. What if he had that future within his grasp and lost it, lost *her*? Losing his father had destroyed his mother. He didn't want that to happen to him, but it could if he let it.

How appropriate the song was.

The singer crooned about how a house was not a home when his love was away. He couldn't help but wonder how Stormclyffe would feel if she left. He'd be alone every night. The thought was unbearable.

He joined her on the floor and pulled her into his arms. Her body bumped into his as she settled against him. They began a slow dance, the gentle shuffle of her flats and his shoes over polished wood. He tucked her head into his shoulder with a gentle hand, and she exhaled softly. Her warm breath seeped into his thin wool sweater.

"I thought you wouldn't be a good dancer since you acted so afraid, but you're excellent," she murmured against his throat.

He smiled. "My father taught me. You form a box with your steps." He demonstrated the incredibly simple move, both their heads bent as they watched their own feet. "And then," he chuckled, "when you become very good, you round off the corners of the box." There were many other fancy dances he was familiar with, but this one, the simple slow dance, was the one his father had taught him, and the one he suspected his father had used when he'd proposed to his mother.

The song changed, and a rich, upbeat melody washed

over them as the sound bounced off the walls around them. She tilted her head back to look up at him with joy.

She started to sing along, laughing at the lyrics and herself.

"'Tiny Dancer' is my dad's favorite song. He and mom always dance to it when they think my brother and I aren't around to see." She blushed and resumed singing. "Hold me closer," she whispered.

He wasn't sure if she was singing the lyrics or pleading to be held tighter. He knew what he wanted and pulled her close so she fit snug against him. One of his hands settled on her lower back, just above the delicious curve of her bottom. In that moment, he was struck by a sense of surreal wonder. It was as though time had in fact stopped and there was nothing beyond the music, Jane, and the dance. He hungered for her both physically and emotionally.

His palm twitched with the urge to cup her bottom, knead it until she mewled with desire and melted against him. His other hand met hers, and he laced their fingers together, the connection sparking between them. They started moving quicker in the dance, and he couldn't help but sing, and she laughed, her smile bright and full of life.

Each time they broke into the refrain, he spun her outward, and she pivoted in a graceful turn like a delicate dancer, using his fingers like the strings of a marionette as though he controlled her perfect moves. The rich sound of the melody and the slide guitar enveloped them in a spell that erased the shadows, the cliffs, like the first wash of the dawn over the land. It overrode the dark, sinister shadows slithering in the corners of the room.

If only he could have danced forever this way, holding her close. He banded his arms around her, fearing the song would end soon. He didn't want to let go of the one real thing in his life. But the music faded, and she pulled back. There was a stark pain in her eyes.

"What's the matter?" He reached for her but she stepped back, holding up a hand.

A new song started playing. It was "Smoke Gets In Your Eyes."

"I can't do this. I shouldn't have." She shook her head.

"Shouldn't what?" he asked. Worry dug into him, making him ache inside.

"I was in a relationship with a guy. We were engaged. I loved him." Her voice broke a little and she drew in a deep breath. "We used to dance all the time. I thought I could handle being close to someone again, but I was wrong." She smiled, but it was one of misery and laced with devastation.

"What happened?" He refused to let her go, not when she was hurting so badly that it made her tremble.

"He didn't believe me. I told him about the dreams, about Stormclyffe. He thought I was crazy. Two years! He just broke it off and asked for his ring back."

Her story stunned him. She'd been with a man she'd loved for two years, was going to marry that fellow, and he'd cried off just because she'd had some nightmares? A man shouldn't abandon a woman over something like that.

"I'm not that man, Jane."

"No," she admitted. "But you don't want to believe me. Sure you said you did, but you don't live with these dreams like I do. They always come, and sooner or later you'll stop wanting to pretend you understand."

He tightened his grip, anger rippling beneath his skin. After everything they'd been through, she didn't trust him?

"I said I believed you were seeing visions. Don't you dare doubt me. I said I'd protect you, and I will."

"It's too much, Bastian…" Her eyes seemed almost blue as unshed tears glimmered in their depths.

Too much? What did she mean? Too much of what?

"Jane, please." He didn't know what he was asking, but he

couldn't bear the thought of her leaving.

She shook her head violently. "You're not supposed to be like this."

"Like what?" Her attempts to pull away from him were baffling.

"Perfect." The single word was barely a whisper from her lips before she spun on her heel and dashed out of the room, leaving him alone on the dance floor.

Something in his chest cracked and splintered. He could almost feel pieces of himself falling apart inside.

The song kept playing, the words a haunting warning.

Love is blind.

He swallowed hard as Jane vanished out of ballroom door.

A fluttering movement in the corner of his eyes made him turn, and his heart jolted. A shadow hung at the edge of the floor, twisting and coiling like a serpent. The darkness stretched up the stone wall, like a thorny vine until it seeped out of the stones and morphed into a figure. Bastian watched in mute fascination as the smoky shape transformed into a handsome man with graying skin and haunted eyes, heavily shadowed with bruises, which locked on Bastian. It looked like the man in the portrait in Jane's room. It looked like... Richard.

"What in God's name?" He stepped toward the man, to do what, he didn't know, but the man shrunk back into a shadow and shot across the floor and through the door, the way Jane had gone. Was he going after her? To hurt her?

"Jane!" he shouted, fear clenching his throat as he broke into a run.

• • •

Tears spilled down her cheeks, drying in salty tracks. Jane

scrubbed at them with her sleeve, her throat constricting as she tried not to cry.

Damn the man! She was completely embarrassed by her reaction to him and how she had just run away like a coward.

It felt too good to be true, to be in his arms, music enveloping her soul, binding her to the handsome Earl of Weymouth. She couldn't be falling in love with him. She had promised herself she wouldn't let this infatuation become anything deeper. After Tim, she hadn't wanted another man to have that power over her, the power to destroy her heart. What a fool she was. She should have known her heart would be the one thing she wouldn't be able to control.

She passed by the red drawing room and froze. A creeping chill slithered up her body from her toes to her head. Like how she'd felt in the library before she'd lost control and walked to the tower to throw herself over.

"Oh God," she murmured through barely parted lips. "Not again."

The drawing room door was barely opened, leaving a sliver of inky darkness. Anything and anybody could have been beyond the door. The thought made her insides squirm and twist sharply. Tiny hairs on her neck and arms rose in warning. The soft sounds of the castle faded to a heavy, blanket-thick silence until a ringing started in her ears.

The blackness of the drawing room seemed to move and stretch, bending rebelliously against the light of the hallway. The lights in the wall sconces flickered, dimmed once, and, in a rush of popping noises, went out.

She sucked in a harsh breath as darkness surrounded her. She couldn't see… Her eyes screamed with the need to focus on something, anything. Why couldn't she move? Her feet were rooted to the floor.

Shhh…shh… The slide of something rasping over of the carpet raked over her sensitive ears.

Shhh…shh…

It sounded like dragging footsteps… Something was coming toward her. Sheer terror spiked through her, and just like that, she was able to move again.

She spun, crashing into the solid stone of a wall. Her whimper was cut short as a high, keening wail drowned her out, like a banshee crying out its warning of a fast-approaching death.

If only I could see… God, just let me see it! She would rather see the creature that approached, look into the face of the thing that was haunting her steps. Not knowing, not seeing, was killing her.

She had the urge to scream Bastian's name, to call for help. But that would just give away her location to the thing that hunted her. His name was on her lips when the choking blackness was cut through by a burst of blue light from inside the drawing room. Desperate to escape the darkened hallway, she rushed into the drawing room.

The setting sun had sunk beneath the sky, and only the moon's wan glow illuminated everything. A pearly light blossomed in the center of the room, floating like a small orb. Tendrils of light spun outward from it in soft, lazy patterns.

The sight mesmerized her, pulling her toward it, leaving her unable to stop. The orb of light moved up to illuminate the portrait of Isabelle. Jane looked from the bottom of the painting upward, studying the silk gown up to the face of the captivating woman who'd died so long ago. Her ancestor. Blood of her blood. Flesh of her flesh.

Twin tracks of blood oozed from Isabelle's eyes, dripping down the oil portrait.

A silent scream knotted in Jane's throat, but that didn't stop her hand from rising up to touch the line of blood. Her fingers came away covered in the ruby substance. The ball of light above her started to spin, moving faster and faster, before it grew bright and shot straight at her. It hit her chest, and her vision tunneled.

Something was inside her! It curled deep into her muscles, and her bones, taking hold of her, ramming against the protective barriers she had in her mind.

This isn't real, this isn't happening.

But it was.

Possession.

"Jane?" Bastian's voice echoed just outside, and she opened her mouth to shout, to warn him, but nothing came out. She stumbled forward a step, running into the back of a chair. Pain shot up her stomach and into her chest from the collision. Something dark and angry inside her clawed for control, fighting to take over.

"Jane?" He stepped into the doorway, eyes locking on her, his face lined with worry. "Jane what's wrong?" He started toward her when a second ball of ghostly light winked into existence behind him.

He spun to face it just as the orb sank into his chest. He went rigid, his entire body jolting before he fell to the floor. Jane tried to reach him, but she tripped and the carpet rose to meet her.

She blinked several times, each more slowly than the last, her final sight was the blood running down the gown of Isabelle's portrait, before darkness closed in.

Richard lounged in a chair by the fire, a glass of brandy in one hand. His coat was gone, his shirt open at the collar, and he was so deep into his cups he didn't care. Nothing mattered anymore.

Isabelle was gone.

Even the happy grin of his infant son, Edward, could not ease the ache in his chest. It was as though someone had ripped his beating heart out and cast it over the cliffs with Isabelle.

He dragged a shaking hand through his hair, mussing it

up further, and took another slow drink of the only thing that seemed to numb his pain.

"My lord, you have a visitor." His butler interrupted his solitude.

"Who is it?" Richard growled. It was dark. He should have no visitors at this hour.

"Miss Cordelia Huntington."

"Bloody hell," Richard growled.

The last woman on earth he wished to see. Before he'd met Isabelle, Cordelia would have been the sort of woman he would have considered marrying.

Pain lanced through him at the simple thought of his wife, carving her name into his heart all over again.

What did Miss Huntington want at this time of night? He ought to send her away from Stormclyffe, but he was foxed, and his mood was black enough he that he longed to get into a row even with a lady.

"Show her in."

"My lord?" His butler's tone was heavy with disapproval, but he didn't care.

"Show her in!"

The butler scowled but exited with a nod and a muttered "Very well."

A few minutes later a woman in a red cloak entered. Her hood concealed her features as she walked around the side of his chair to face him. She dropped her hood, revealing honey-blond hair and a beautiful face with the coldest hazel eyes he'd ever seen. Richard shuddered as her gaze fixed on him. He didn't bother to stand as he ought to in a lady's presence. He just didn't give a damn.

"What brings you here, Miss Huntingdon?" he growled at her, hoping to drive her away with crudeness. He wanted to mourn Isabelle in peace.

"You do, my lord. I thought it was time to point out that

you are in need of a wife. I offer myself to you. My father is quite wealthy and—"

"Silence." The word came out sharp as a whip crack. He couldn't believe this woman. She thought to marry him? When his heart was destroyed and his soul ripped to pieces?

"The only woman I loved is gone, and you think I care for riches?"

Her plump red lips thinned into an angry line. "It is time you settled down with a woman worthy of your title. My great-grandfather on my mother's side was an earl. I am much better suited to the role of countess than some innkeeper's daughter."

He jumped to his feet and threw his glass of brandy in the fireplace. The explosion of glass and the rush of flames consuming the alcohol forced Cordelia back a step.

"You insult her; you insult me. Know this, Miss Huntington. I will never marry again."

She curled her lip in an unladylike sneer. "You will marry. It is your duty to carry on your line. And I will provide you with an heir."

He laughed harshly. "I have my son, Edward."

"A child with a dirty, common bloodline?"

He wrapped a hand around her throat the second she uttered the words. "Never insult my son again." He released her and shoved her away from him so he could pace over to the window and gaze out upon the night.

The soft clink *of glasses and the trickle of liquid was soon followed by her coming to his side.*

"My apologies, my lord. I've spoken rashly and out of turn. Here…drink this. It will calm your nerves." She placed a brandy glass in his hand.

With a vicious glare at her, he downed the liquid and set the glass on the windowsill. He licked his lips. The brandy tasted a little bitter.

"It's a pity you couldn't be made to come around." She

stroked his cheek.

Her touch burned like cold fire against his skin. He slapped her hand away, and the room spun slightly, blurring at the edges of his vision.

"You should leave, Miss Huntington. The hour is late, and you will be missed." The last few words of his speech slurred as his tongue grew heavy and thick.

She laughed quietly, yet the sound seemed more sharp and piercing to his ears, as though they strained to pick up every sound around him.

"I will leave... As soon as I've watched the last breath leave your body, and then I will go upstairs and take your precious babe and throw him off the cliffs like I did the common whore who birthed him." The venom in her tone was pure acid to his ears.

He spun to face her, using the windowsill to support himself as his legs quaked beneath him.

"What? You mean...she didn't kill herself?" Through the murky waters of his mind, this revelation was strangely a comfort. Months of guilt had driven him to the bottle, had him ignoring his son. And now he'd learned Isabelle hadn't committed suicide?

"I cast a spell upon her." She explained the murder with all the casual disinterest of someone discussing the weather. "I'm a witch, you see. My mother taught me well. The hearts of a dozen innocent doves taken by force beneath a full moon gave me the power to enslave your darling wife's free will. I forced her to flee into the storm and come to the cliffs. And when she arrived, I shoved her over the edge." Her pupils appeared almost catlike, and Richard shook his head, trying to make sense of what she was saying.

"Why? Why kill her?" he demanded hoarsely.

Shock numbed Richard. His throat started to close.

"It's not just her I've killed... I've poisoned your brandy.

Feeling short of breath yet?" As she spoke, she slid one hand into the folds of her cloak and retrieved a vial filled with red liquid. She uncapped the stopper and smeared the liquid along her palm.

He doubled over, coughing as he struggled to breathe.

"I was the proper choice as your wife. But you picked that woman. That innkeeper's daughter!" She lunged for him, smearing the liquid...blood...on his chest.

"It was my choice. I loved her," he choked out, shoving her hands away from him.

"You shamed me by picking her. And now I shall have my revenge on you all."

Her eyes glowed, orange flames destroying any glimmer of humanity that might have remained there.

"I'll take great pleasure in tossing that brat into the sea for the fish to devour. Tenebrosum cor tuum anima vestra, et tenebrarum. Tu mihi in sempiternum. Masculi Omnia mihi." She smiled at him, the expression full of pure malice. "Everyone in your family will suffer. This will never be the end, not until I own the soul of an heir to Stormclyffe."

Something deep within Richard refused to die, even as the poison spread through him, killing him.

This bitch would not kill his son!

He shoved away from the window and tackled her. His hands wrapped around her throat. Even as his strength began to fail and his vision blurred, he kept hold of her, squeezing. He heard the faint cry of his little boy one floor above. The sound infused him with one last burst of determination and power.

"You will never harm another soul, never take another life!" He squeezed again, and the flames in her eyes were extinguished. His heart gave out, and he slumped forward.

Chapter Fourteen

Bastian jerked awake, gasping for breath. His mind reeled with what he'd just seen. Had it been real? A witch named Cordelia Huntington had murdered Isabelle and Richard? Could he believe what he'd seen? Or had it been merely fevered imaginings?

Head pounding, he glanced around the drawing room. Jane was sprawled facedown a few feet away.

She stirred and groaned. "Bastian, I had the strangest dream…" She looked around, confused. "Why are we on the floor?"

"Jane, did you see…?" He struggled to find the words.

"Richard and Cordelia? Yes, front-row seat and everything." She sat up and shoved her hair back from her face, her lips drawn tight in a grim line. After a moment, her lips softened, parted, and she drew a slow breath before continuing. "Honestly, I'm so scared I want to run for the nearest door, but…"

"But?" he echoed. Odd how he hoped this one little word meant she wouldn't leave him.

"Well, I can't leave you here alone. You are a disaster waiting to happen, Bastian. I bet you'd walk into a dark cellar without a second thought as to what's down there."

His lips twitched. "Like bottles of wine? That's all that's in my cellars."

She raised a single brow. "That you know of. This is exactly why I have to stay. You don't have the good sense to leave. Someone has to watch over you. It would really piss me off if some ghosts got the better of you because you won't admit they exist."

Bastian got to his feet and helped Jane up, holding her close. "I know you don't trust me, but I believe you. This is real. You were right."

She studied him, seeming to search for any sign or hint of deception. "Really? You don't think I'm crazy then?"

He shook his head. "No. Enough has happened to prove you were right. We're facing something supernatural, and I'm not arguing with you anymore."

Her shoulders sagged and she sighed with relief. "Thank God, because trying to protect someone who doesn't believe in ghosts is usually how people die in bad horror movies."

He chuckled. "Jane, this is real life, not a movie."

She raised one challenging brow. "Exactly. All the more reason to be careful and keep you out of trouble."

"Are you braving potentially malignant spirits because you care about me?"

He had to admit he rather liked the idea of this little American firecracker of a woman coming to his defense. Even though he could protect himself, especially from incorporeal creatures, he enjoyed seeing her flushed with excitement, eyes bright with her determination to save him. If only he could get her to take that same passion to a bed, preferably his.

"Don't look so smug. I'm here because it's my duty to find out the truth. My dissertation needs to be flawless, all my research a hundred percent accurate before I present it."

Her rigid back and crossed arms showed a defiance he hadn't expected, and it aroused him. He couldn't help but wonder if he could get her to submit to him, if she'd agree to being tied…

"Hey! Eyes on my face." She waved a hand in front of his eyes, getting him to look up from her lovely breasts. "Clearly my hunch was right. Isabelle was murdered, and now we know that Richard was as well by a woman named Cordelia Huntington. No wonder this place is haunted. I'd be angry if everyone thought my wife killed herself and then I got murdered by the same maniac who killed my wife. I bet Richard is roaming the halls at night just like Isabelle does the cliffs."

Bastian's hands around her waist tightened. "What makes you think Isabelle haunts the cliffs?" Another secret she had been keeping from him?

She licked her lips nervously. "I—I saw her when I first arrived. You haven't seen her?"

"No. I've never seen anything in this house before today. There were rumors of course, other people seeing her, but I haven't witnessed her or anything else before you arrived. What did she look like?"

"She was dressed in a white gown. She flowed over the earth and straight to the cliffs." She paused, her gaze distant, voice soft as though recalling a sad memory. "She turned back to look at me. Her eyes…so full of sadness. I wanted to help her, Bastian. I *have* to help her."

He caught an errant lock of her hair, coiling it around his finger. "So I'm never to be rid of you?" He phrased it as though she was a nuisance but his kept his tone soft, hoping she'd sense he meant the opposite.

He tugged on the gleaming coil, reveling in its silkiness. She was just so touchable. Everything about Jane from her pale pink lips to her silky hair and full curves demanded he touch her.

"I'm not going anywhere until we figure this business out," she vowed.

God, he loved it when she did that. No one and nothing would deter his little bookworm from getting her way.

"So…if Richard killed Cordelia but died at the same time, why was the discovery of her body not mentioned along with Richard's when a footman found him? Surely the local authorities would have investigated and reported another body. In all my sources I only ever came across the discovery of his body. No one ever mentioned poison."

He tucked one of her arms in his as they left the drawing room. "I've never even heard of this woman before now."

She glanced at him. "I have. She's in the diary. It's just like in the…" She hesitated before continuing. "In the vision. Cordelia was hanging around Richard, hoping to marry him, but he met Isabelle, and the rest was history. Apparently there's more to this woman than Richard knew, if what we saw was true. She was some sort of witch, or practiced witchcraft at least. It all comes back to the murdered doves. There were several places in the diary where Richard mentioned the birds dying. I think she was must have been sacrificing them to cast her spells. She said something right before Richard died, something that sounded like Latin. I think I can write it down, and we can translate it later. I bet it was a spell."

He sighed. "Are we really talking spells and witchcraft? All of that *Macbeth* nonsense with women over smoking cauldrons?"

She patted his arm reassuringly, even though there was a mocking light in her eyes. "Just because you're afraid to accept there are things beyond what you can understand doesn't mean those things don't actually exist. I think, given everything that's happened, we have to entertain the possibility that we are in fact dealing with witches and spells."

"And the body we found in the garden?" he asked as they ascended the grand staircase together.

"Cordelia's. I'm certain of it. We saw the remnants of a red cloak in the grave, remember? She was wearing that in the vision we saw."

"Very well, I give you that much." He had to agree that it was too much of a coincidence otherwise. "We should go to town tomorrow and look through the archives and see if we can track down Cordelia. We'll wait until Randolph returns. He can watch over the workmen."

"Sounds like a plan."

When Jane reached her room, she glanced up at him through her sooty lashes.

"After what just happened…do you feel fine sleeping alone?" Her cheeks flushed and her gaze flicked away from his face.

He picked up on her hesitation and wondered what he was supposed to do. She'd made it clear she wasn't ready for a relationship, that she'd been wounded before and couldn't trust another man right now. What did she want him to do? "I do, but if *you* don't…"

Before he could even finish, she had snatched her bag and was marching into his room as though she belonged there.

"Great, thanks! You want the right or left side? Whoa, this bed is massive."

She dropped her bags and circled his bed, her gray eyes wider than usual. "Plenty of room…for two." A delectable blush tiptoed across her cheeks as she stroked her palm over the velvet coverlet with a wistful gaze clouding her eyes.

He wondered what she was thinking about. Did she want to be in bed with him as much as he wanted her beneath him, begging for more, crying out for him? Ever since he'd kissed her in the drawing room, he felt that things had been building to this. But he didn't want her in his bed because she was afraid. Even that was too low for a man hungry to kiss every inch of her as he was. If she shared his bed, it should be because she wanted him, not because she was terrified of being alone.

"Jane, I'm sorry you've become involved in this, but I'm glad you're here. Had I been dealing with this alone…I do not know what would have happened." It was as close as he could come to confessing he was also glad he wasn't alone.

She offered him a rueful smile. "Lucky for you the ghost seems to want *me* dead, not you." She paused, voice breaking. He moved to her and eased her down on the bed, tucking her safely against his side.

"I'm sorry." He meant it. If he had known she'd be so affected staying here, he would have dragged her out to her rental car and driven her back to town himself. He didn't want to lose another person he cared about to the madness that haunted this place. History couldn't repeat itself.

"It's fine, really. I just wish I didn't believe in all of this stuff, but I do. Blame my parents for raising me a God-fearing Catholic, but I believe in ghosts a hundred percent." As she spoke she touched a small medallion around her neck, her thumb and forefinger rubbing over the image of an archangel slaying a dragon.

She lifted her head and looked toward the large window closest to her. Even in her fear she was beautiful.

His throat tightened as he recalled his mother's change after his father never returned from Stormclyffe. How she used to sit in a large, overstuffed chair by the window in their house outside London, her cheek resting on the sun-bleached fabric as her forlorn stare swept the garden outside the window. His mother seemed so far away, as though she'd traveled to a distant land and hadn't ever truly returned. She was haunted by losing her husband.

No. She wouldn't go the way his mother had. He wouldn't

lose another person to this cursed pile of stones.

He directed his gaze back to Jane, admiring her. She was so lovely. There was a quiet, yet untamed ferocity in her, driven by her passions and tempered by her determination. People didn't act like she did anymore. They didn't have strength. They didn't fight against their fears to help others. Such a woman was rare.

Am I falling in love?

Previously, he would have laughed at the notion. But at this moment, alone in a bedroom with her, he thought it was possible to be in love with Jane. There was nothing false about her, no secrets she wouldn't reveal to him if he took the time to delve into her soul. He could trust her, could be himself with her without fear of anything. He'd danced and sung with her, let her see inside himself where he'd never let another woman in. She'd accepted him as he was, weaknesses and fears alike and had liked him, more than liked him. It was impossible not to love someone who made you feel like that.

Even though he'd known her a short time, it made perfect sense. You could wait a lifetime hoping to earn someone's trust and love, but sometimes…it happened fast and unexpected like the shock of a doorknob when crossing the carpet in socks. The jolt of instant realization, the sign that something was meant to be, that you belonged to another person. He couldn't deny it. He belonged to Jane, whether she knew it or not, whether she wanted him or not.

She sidled closer to him, nibbling on her bottom lip.

"What can I do to ease your worries, Jane?" He acted without thinking, lips brushing a kiss on her temple. She shivered hard and turned into him, burying her face in his sweater. Bastian shook his head in a silent laugh. Three days ago he'd been obsessed with restoring Stormclyffe and nothing else. Now that barely mattered in comparison to protecting Jane from angry spirits.

Tomorrow, he would take her to town and let her relax. As much as he wanted her to stay here, she needed to go, needed to stay clear of the shadows that lingered in Stormclyffe's halls.

"Come on, let's get ready for bed. I don't know about you, but I've been up since before dawn and would love to catch up on my sleep." He separated himself from her and saw the look of regret on her face.

"I'm so sorry. I've been crying and acting like such a ninny."

"Everybody gets scared. Even me," he declared with a teasing stoicism.

She laughed. "I don't think I ever want to encounter what makes you scared. Does anything frighten you?"

Losing the people I love. Rather than admit that aloud, he shrugged.

"I'm human, just like everyone else."

Her nose crinkled with a little smile. "Sometimes I think it would be nice to be superhuman. Where's a radioactive spider when you need one?"

He cocked a brow as though her reference was entirely lost on him even though he knew what she was talking about.

Half amused, half exasperated, she explained. "Oh come on. You know, Spiderman? The superhero? Didn't you read comic books as a kid? Living with a brother, I know way more about this stuff than I should probably admit."

Her sheepish grin made his heart turn over in his chest. "I spent most of my childhood feeling like a bit of an outcast. Given my family's unique history, I was lucky I wasn't bullied, much." He winced at the unwanted memories. Boys were notorious for wanting to ostracize those who were different, especially those with family histories that were less than normal. "There was the occasional skirmish but I always held my own. It was difficult though, since I was small for my age."

Her brows arched up in surprise. "You, small? I can't picture that, you're so muscled and strong…"

Her eyes darkened with desire as she raked her gaze over his body, and it made his own lust stir in response. She was so dangerous, and she didn't even know it.

"Thank you for the compliment." He chuckled. "I didn't really start to grow until my last few years at Eton."

She blushed. "I meant to say…"

He waved a hand and offered her a reassuring smile.

"Well, you ought to use the bathroom first. I'll just change clothes." He could practically feel the blush in his face, the creeping heat as she bashfully looked away, too.

And to think I was so good at this before.

She had the audacity to giggle. "This is going to be so awkward, isn't it?"

"I don't normally have issues with women," he confessed.

Her face turned a charming shade of red, and she glanced away. She said something, but he didn't hear her. All he could focus on was her pink tongue darting out nervously to wet those succulent lips. Lust swirled in dark edges in the center of his soul. He'd give anything to drag her into his arms and possess that sweet little mouth. Burn away all the fear she'd felt in the last few days and turn her world inside out with mind-numbing pleasure…

She unzipped her suitcase and pulled out silk-striped pajamas. She darted off to the bathroom, and the door clicked shut behind her. He stifled a groan as he tried to walk, but his erection was determined to punch through the front of his trousers. He reached his dresser and dug around until he found some heavy flannel pajamas for himself. He doubted she would have handled the news very well if he'd told her he normally slept in the nude. Wearing some barriers of clothes would keep his behavior in check tonight. He hoped. He didn't want to be that man who took advantage of a woman feeling vulnerable.

It was a cold night, but he'd sleep shirtless because he was burning up with completely inappropriate arousal. He flipped the metal clasp of his wristwatch open, slid it off, and set it on the dresser. He considered it. The watch was a handsome piece, expensive like everything else he owned. Rich in wealth, poor in family. A curse he could not escape.

Despite the tragedy of his family's history, they'd always prospered financially. It was like a devil's bargain. And he was starting to despise the money. He'd rather have his father back than the Aston Martin in the front drive.

He moved to the window. He scanned the hillside that sloped down from the castle to the shores. A white shape drifted from the rose covered archway of the garden below and continued toward the cliffs.

A trick of the moonlight, a play of shadows perhaps? It couldn't be what it appeared to be…a woman in a flowing white gown. He fancied he saw the figure look over her shoulder at the castle. Another shift of light, a flicker of shadow, and a second figure materialized in the garden archway. A feminine figure wearing a red cloak. Two white, perfect little hands dropped the hood away from the figure's head. The head was only a rotting skull with bits of hair straggling down off the yellowish bone. The figure turned to face the window, and its sunken eye sockets were black pits reflecting the emptiness, the decay of his family's history, his own soul.

He stumbled away from the window, horror ripping through his insides. Before he could even process what he'd just seen, Jane's scream split through the haze of shock that had enveloped him.

Chapter Fifteen

Jane stripped her clothes off, admiring the expensive Italian marble bathroom. The shower had a walk-in entry and was large enough to hold five people. There was a marble bench opposite the huge shower nozzle. She tiptoed into the stall and turned on the water. The initial blast was cold, and mist formed a layer of dew on her skin. When the water was hot and steam filled the shower, fogging all the mirrors and doors, she ducked under the spray.

The heat was intoxicating, and she closed her eyes. Her hands rubbed, massaged, and slid over her body, her breasts, down her thighs. The warmth of the water lulled her into a dreamy state of lust. She leaned back against the shower wall, indulging in a fantasy of Bastian. It was his hands cupping her breasts, pinching her nipples. His mouth drew one aching peak between his lips, sucking hard in long pulls that had her fisting her hands in his hair to urge him on.

Smack!

A big shampoo bottle hit the floor and rolled toward the drain. She swallowed several times, trying to force her heart back down from where it had jumped into her throat. She bent over, picked the bottle up, and set it in the stall corner. When she raised her head and looked through the glass shower door, she screamed.

A face stared back at her through the steam. A face that was more bone than flesh, with eyes of flames and blood oozing down its bony cheeks. Strips of hair still clung to the partially decayed scalp, in long greasy tendrils. Even over the sound of rushing water, the creature's ragged breaths scraped over Jane's ears.

Hehhhhh.

Hehhhhh.

The rasping death rattle invaded her mind, challenging every instinct she had to scream.

The creature raised a skeletal finger and carved a word into the steam on the glass.

Mine.

Trails of dark, brownish blood dribbled from the word, mixing with the steam's moisture until pink rivulets trickled down the shower door.

Air flooded Jane's lungs, and she screeched. The figure vanished at the same moment Bastian burst through the bathroom door.

"What happened?"

"Oh, God! Bastian, it was here. It was right here!" She pointed at the door, but the word and the blood were gone. Her mind whirled, trying to make sense of what she'd just seen and how it was possible that it had vanished in the next instant.

"What? I don't see anything." His gaze roved over the room, taking in everything with a guarded and protective stare.

"Great, I'm losing it," she mumbled. Her whole body shook so badly she collapsed in the shower.

He peered through the door at her. "Are you all right? I'm coming in."

The soft *thud* of shoes hitting the marble told her he was joining her. She tucked her knees up to her chin and wrapped her arms around her shins, hiding her nakedness. Despite the chills racking her body, her face still flamed at the thought of him climbing into the shower with her. Rather than strip down, he walked in, slacks, sweater, and all. He cranked the nozzle to make the water even hotter and sat down next to her on the floor, ignoring the fact that he was getting soaked.

"What are you doing? You'll ruin your clothes," she mumbled.

"Doesn't matter." He slid his other arm around her shoulders, tucking her against him.

"What happened?" His warm breath slid over her forehead as he placed a kiss on her temple.

She repressed a shiver of longing.

"It was a ghost. A decaying, rotting thing. It wrote the word 'mine' in the steam." She wiped at the tears pooling in the corners of her eyes. She'd never known such fear before, facing true evil. She knew that's what it was. *Evil.* And it terrified her. Seeing Isabelle on the cliff hadn't scared her, it only made her sad. This…this creature in the bathroom. That hadn't been like Isabelle. It was pure evil.

"I believe you. I saw it, too…only it was outside in the garden. It was…"—He hesitated— "Chasing Isabelle to the cliffs. It stopped and looked up at me and…" This time he didn't continue.

"Even though the body's gone…she's still here. Cordelia is still here. Just like Isabelle said." She shivered. "What are we going to do? How do you get rid of a ghost? Should we call a priest and have an exorcism?"

"I don't know. She's gone for now. Don't let her frighten you. I'm here with you, Jane. She can't touch you while I'm here."

She wanted to believe him, and he made it so easy to. He was strong and brave, even if a bit close-minded about ghosts. Of course, he was starting to believe her now. He was seeing things too, and that was bad news because it meant what they were seeing was real.

He caught her hand and brought it to his lips, sucking her index finger into his mouth. It was the perfect distraction, replacing her terror with sexual hunger.

Damn the man, he was too perfect. Heat pooled between her thighs, and she leaned into him, watching his lips move around her finger. He released her finger and raised his eyes to hers. The faintest glimmer of a shadow flitted past his irises.

"Kiss me, Jane." His gruff tone made her body quiver deliciously.

There was no thinking after that, only action. She turned in his arms, her lips seeking his. They shared a groan as her breasts pressed against his chest. She gripped the bottom of his sweater and tore it off him. He pulled her onto her feet, and she kissed him while he rid himself of his slacks and boxers. He kissed back in playful, aggressive nibbles that had her body flashing between his heat and the press of cool marble behind her.

He growled when her exploring hands brushed his straining cock. She glanced down, eyes widening at his impressive length. *There is no way...*

"You can take me, Jane. You can take all of me."

His hungry gaze raked over her bare breasts and between her thighs. A look so possessive, so hot she could actually feel it on her skin.

He ran his hands up and down her arms, soothing her. She licked her lips, craving to taste him, her body screaming for his. Without another word, he gripped her waist and pulled her flush against him. His cock nestled against her belly, and he thrust his tongue between her lips, owning her mouth. He guided her back against the shower wall, cupping her ass, lifted her, and shoved a knee between her thighs, spreading her open. When he broke the kiss to gaze down at her center, she blushed scarlet and tried to close her legs. Vulnerability blazed in her, making her weak and scared of what he might think.

"You're so beautiful." He parted her folds with one finger, tracing heated patterns in the sensitive flesh.

She trembled and gripped his shoulders for support. He was undoing all of her defenses with that wicked touch.

"Do you want me inside you? I'll make love to you, slow, hard. I'll part this soft flesh, drive inside you until you scream… Do you want that?" The edge to his tone only made her wetter. She loved that he gave into his passion completely.

The ferocity etched in his handsome features made her whimper with need. She needed his raw passion, needed his animal lust to take over. He placed himself at her entrance, waited for her impatient nod and shoved inside.

His first thrust was fast and hard, everything he promised. She threw her head back and arched away from the wall as he withdrew and slammed home. The sensation of him filling her, merging their bodies in an explosion of bliss caught her completely unprepared. Had sex ever felt like this? Like heaven and earth and every breathless second in between?

"Bastian!" His name was a breathless prayer on her lips. A plea for more.

His hands dug into her hips as he held her still for his ramming hips.

The hiss of water around them and rhythmic sounds of their flesh striking together was so hot that she panted, her body on fire and restless with the need to come. Her heels sank into his lower back, holding him to her. He snarled and dropped his head to her neck, sinking his teeth in her skin to hold her in place. The rough love bite sent her over the edge.

An orgasm burst through her, flooding her senses with a euphoria of dark, sinful pleasure. She surrendered to the riptide of sensations and slumped against the wall. He kept thrusting, little feral growls escaping his throat, vibrating against her neck, making her body ripple with mini-orgasms.

He came with a roar, pressing deep inside her. He rolled his hips tight against hers, riding out his own pleasure, as though determined to keep them as close as possible. His forehead rested against hers as they shared breath, eyes closed.

"Bloody hell…Jane…" He groaned. "I didn't think about protection. I just lost my mind when I kissed you."

She stroked his face with her fingertips, making his eyelashes fan open. "It's okay. I'm on the pill." She nibbled his lower lip. "I like that you lost control."

Hot water pelted his back and shoulders, and she leaned forward to lick the beading droplets off his skin. He shifted and groaned softly as though agonized by the ecstasy of her tongue on his flesh. There was something wildly intimate about that moment. Nothing between them, no secrets. Just two beating hearts in time and the comfort of human touch.

He cleared his throat. "Jane, I'm sorry I took advantage…"

She captured his lips, silencing the unnecessary apology. She offered him her acceptance by stroking his hair, his back, any part of him she could reach.

"I wanted that more than you," she murmured against his lips.

He smiled crookedly and took one of her nipples between his thumb and forefinger, tweaking it until she gasped in pleasure and arched. His cock jerked to life inside her.

"I wouldn't make that bet, darling."

"Oh?" Her lashes fluttered open. *Surely he didn't mean…*

"I've had only the most wicked thoughts about you. I'm betting a few of them are illegal in some countries."

His teasing tone and the carnal promise of his words had her clit pulsing and her legs shaking with anticipation. Little aftershocks of pleasure kept rippling through her as he continued to play with her, sweet, gentle, but no less seductive.

"You're a genuine bad boy, eh?" She laughed, trying not to squirm as he rocked into her, their bodies still connected.

He dropped a kiss on the tip of her nose. "More than you know."

• • •

Bastian insisted on properly washing her, and it wasn't just an excuse to keep touching her. That was merely a bonus. Truthfully, he needed to care for her. She'd been through so much since coming here, and he felt somehow responsible.

She leaned back against him as he soaped her body. Her surrender was amazing. She was willing to trust him completely with her body. His past relationships had been with volatile, passionate, and wild women, and he'd enjoyed the roller coaster. Jane was different. She was sweet, curious, passionate, and trusting. All it took was one look from her bedroom eyes, and he had trouble keeping control of his own release. He'd taken her raw, dirty, and rough, and she'd had the audacity to smile like a sleepy kitten and nuzzle him afterward.

"You're quite a woman, Jane." He licked the delicate shell of her ear.

She answered with a shivery little sigh, her lashes fanning out across her cheeks as she closed her eyes.

He turned her in his arms and kissed her, his hands sliding down the slope of her back and over her backside. She arched into him, an invitation to take what he desperately needed.

"Round two?" he asked between kisses.

"I demand nothing less." She laughed breathlessly.

Without another word, he swept her back over his arm, trailing kisses down her neck to her breasts. Taking time to explore the tender peaks with his teeth and tongue, he delighted in the little moans and gasps she made as he bit and sucked on each nipple. Her hands roamed his shoulders before stopping in his hair, tugging fiercely on the strands when he played a little rough with her breasts.

When neither of them could stand another minute of his sensual torture, he backed them up so he could sit on the bench in the shower, the hot spray covering them.

"Straddle me," he growled as he pulled her down on his lap.

"I've never done…" She blushed but he captured her mouth with his, distracting her from her embarrassment before he showed her how to guide him into her body. She hissed softly when she took him all the way inside.

"Oh God!" She threw her head back, her breasts thrust out like tantalizing offerings and he couldn't resist.

He threaded his fingers through her hair, tugging gently on the strands to keep her head back and her breasts close to his mouth. With urging from his hips, she soon learned to ride him in a wild rhythm that wound him so tight and kept him so hard he couldn't remember his name. There was nothing beyond the ecstasy of being with her, feeling her silken sheath wrapped around him, her cries filling his ears. When they flew apart in each others' arms, he saw something so deep, so pure in her eyes that it stopped time. For a second he couldn't breathe, couldn't speak, he simply stared back, lost in her gaze, hoping he reflected back what he was feeling and seeing in her eyes.

"Bastian…" His name trembled off her lips before she buried her face in his neck, pressing light kisses on his skin.

"Jane," he whispered back, her name a midnight prayer.

Neither of them said anything more as they cleaned

themselves again. It was Jane who finally broke the silence.

"What are we going to do about Cordelia?"

He shut off the water, helped her out of the shower, and then wrapped her in a white, fluffy towel. He ignored her question, not wanting to answer it, and covered her head with the towel.

She freed her face from the towel with an irritated little huff and glared.

"Well?"

"Could we table this discussion? Or better yet, can I just have sex with you on the table? That's a much better idea. I did promise to ravish you after all."

He smiled as her eyelids dropped to half-mast and she licked her lips. Then she seemed to come back to herself.

"Seriously, we have to come up with a plan. We can't just sit around and let her pick us off one by one. Not doing anything about a ghost is how horror movies start." She turned her back on him and stalked out of the bathroom. She put on her pj's, covering up all that delectable skin he hadn't yet tasted.

"We will have a plan. Tomorrow." He followed her into the bedroom.

"We might be dead by then." Her tone dripped with sarcasm, but the effect was lessened by the cute way she shrugged her shoulders and finished buttoning her top. The move appeared effortless, casual, but when she caught him watching, her cheeks flushed, and she ducked her face bashfully.

"We won't be. You've been watching too many horror movies." He gripped the collar of her top. "Tomorrow we'll find out more about Cordelia Huntington."

When her eyes narrowed with obvious skepticism, he tugged her to him, kissing her. It was a much-needed diversion for them both. His tongue danced with hers, melting the chill of the night, and she relaxed in his arms. Her soft lips erased the awful memory of seeing that phantom with the rotting face in the garden.

He clutched her harder, using her healing sensuality to rescue himself from the brink of madness. That's what this was.

Madness.

It was insane to fall for a nosy American who was determined to write a dissertation on his family. Insane to think he could restore a castle when his workforce jumped at every shadow. But the worst part was that he'd seen things he couldn't explain. The figure in the garden, the woman in the white dress who vanished over a cliff, and that vision in the drawing room.

The shield of disbelief he erected as a small boy against the darkness and the monsters crumbled against the evidence there was more in the shadows than he wanted to believe.

Ghosts do exist.

When she wrapped her arms tight about his waist and sighed against his throat, he knew it was time to sleep. He lifted her into his arms, enjoying her feminine gasp of surprise as he set her down in his bed.

When he straightened, his body blocked out the light from the window, shrouding Jane in darkness. Moonlight tread around him on cat's paws, unable to reach her. An ancient primal fear rose within him at the sight of her, as though his soul recognized she was in danger.

"Bastian?" She opened her arms to him, inviting him to join her. The fortress of stone guarding his heart shuddered and quaked against her sweet entreaty.

"Hold me." She waved her hands, begging him to move closer.

The walls inside him crumbled like those of Jericho after a trumpet call. He climbed into bed and wrapped his body around hers. He buried his face in her wet hair, the peppermint-tea aroma of his shampoo became a new drug to his system.

Am I lost? Can one lose one's soul to another?

"Yes…" The reply came back in a silvery voice, faded by death and centuries.

Bastian's eyes flew open, scanning the room for an intruder.

It was empty, save for himself and Jane.

Chapter Sixteen

The following morning, Jane couldn't believe she was staring at the most expensive car money could buy. An Aston Martin sat in the drive outside Stormclyffe's front door.

"That's your car?"

"You like it?" Bastian tossed the keys at her.

They bounced off her chest and hit the ground with a heavy *clink*.

"Like it? I think I want to steal it! No wonder you can't go into town unnoticed." She snatched up the keys and gazed at the Aston Martin with sheer lust. It was a model One-77, a gray, two-seat coupe. What person in her right mind wouldn't like it?

"You want to drive?" He pointed at the keys in her hands, the wind teasing his dark blond hair and playfully blowing it in his eyes.

She wanted to hold onto this moment forever. The picture of him smiling, leaning one hip casually against a car almost as sexy as he was, with the sea behind him.

In her hand she held the car keys, but it seemed like the

keys to something more. A dream. Yet here she was living in a haunted castle and sleeping with a veritable sex god with a tender heart. Living a dream. It didn't matter that Bastian hid that softness with an exterior of arrogance. She'd broken through to him, and the man beneath was unbelievable.

I'm falling for him, and he could break my heart. What if, after all of this is over, he doesn't want me? She'd never really known rejection until Tim. And once stung with that sort of pain, she couldn't erase the phantom ache being abandoned left behind. If she fell in love with Bastian and he didn't return those feelings, it would crush her. She wasn't sure she could survive a second time. It was why she'd fought so hard to keep her distance, and yet it hadn't worked. They'd been pulled together like a moon and planet, gravity knotting them into each other's orbit. Inescapable. What would happen when they broke apart?

"Are you well, Jane?" His graceful stride toward her was panther-like. He cupped her face, thumbs brushing away her tears. "Don't cry. Please…" His voice was a gruff whisper. "Whatever is causing those tears, don't think about it. This will all be over soon."

Her eyes shut, and he kissed her lips, holding her tight for a long moment.

"I'll drive," he whispered.

She nodded, desperately focusing on the research ahead of them. She had to forget that her time with him would end. That the irrevocable change he wrought within her would mark her forever as his, but she'd never have him. He'd said it himself. It would all be over soon. It meant he didn't want her, not enough to ask her to stay. This was nothing more than a temporary fling, an intense hookup of two people under a lot of stress. No emotions, no feelings, just sex. And for him it would be over soon. The words were like iron nails in a coffin of the last surviving piece of hope her heart clung to that she could ever be in love with someone who loved her back. Never again.

• • •

An hour later, Jane and Bastian were holed up in an empty study room of the Weymouth library, with a huge stack of books on Stormclyffe and copies of the birth and death records from the surrounding parishes. They'd poured over every bit of history they could find about Bastian's family including the wedding announcement for Richard and Isabelle and the birth record of baby Edward.

After everything she'd experienced with the visions and the diary, she felt connected to the doomed lovers, and reading about their lives had made her heart clench. Such love and happiness—all of it ruined because of one woman's jealousy and greed. Bastian had been there with her through the entire research, his fingers laced through hers. Every now and then he leaned over and pressed a kiss to her temple. He dug deeper and deeper into her heart, leaving her no hope of ever living without him in her life again, but she'd have to when he ended it between them.

Bastian's cell phone buzzed against the wooden library table. He picked it up and then looked at her.

"A colleague of mine, an expert in Latin translations texted me what you wrote down."

Her heart gave a painful thump against her ribs and a knot of fear seemed to solidify in her stomach.

"What did Cordelia's words mean? It was a spell, right?" She knew it had to be.

Bastian glanced down at the screen. "Let your heart be filled with darkness and shadows consume your soul. You belong to me for all eternity. All male heirs shall be mine."

"Whoa." For a second Jane just let the words sink in.

"That sounds like a spell to me. The part that worries me is the male heirs. It's like she was marking your entire family, not just Richard. Every man since him has had some sort of tragedy. Lovers, wives, children of the heirs have all been lost tragically or horrifically." The evidence was in those records she'd examined her first day.

"If it is a spell, shouldn't there be a way to break it?" he asked, frowning.

"That's what I was thinking." Jane nodded. "But it's not like Cordelia left us a handy little *Guide to Being an Evil Witch* lying around. We don't know what we have to do to stop her."

"Or do we?" Bastian sat up straighter. "What once was broken must be mended. Maybe we have to fix the castle. It's what my father tried to do; it's what I'm trying to do. The need to fix it is almost bone-deep, Jane. Like I *have* to do it."

She pursed her lips and considered it. Fixing a castle? It didn't seem like a logical way to break a curse, but then again, this was her first curse to break so she wasn't sure how to go about it.

"Let's finish researching here, before we decide what to do about the spell. We still need to figure out more about her body after she died and how it ended up in your garden."

"Very well." He thumbed idly through the pages of a book, then suddenly froze. He flattened the book open and spun it around for her to see.

"Here." He tapped a section.

She read it aloud. "The year 1811 marked one of the darkest hours in Weymouth. The fifth Earl of Weymouth and his wife suffered tragic deaths. But theirs was not the only tragedy. Cordelia Huntington, daughter of a local gentleman in the village, mysteriously disappeared around the same night the earl died. Her body was never found, and she was presumed dead seven years later."

"What happened to her body?" He shut the book.

"I don't know. Someone had to have moved it from the castle. The question is who?" She slid back in her chair desperately trying to think. "I assume it was one of Richard's servants. They would have seen two bodies in that room and probably disposed of Cordelia's." She closed her eyes, envisioning the scene again.

"If they were anything like Randolph is to me," he noted, "they might have wanted to keep scandal away from Richard's family and taken Cordelia's body and buried it in the garden."

Shuffling her papers and sliding them back into her bag, she turned to him. "That's true. I just wish the articles on Richard's body being found had mentioned who found him. None of them mentioned a person by name."

He rose. "I suppose I'll have to figure that out some other way.

"What do you mean?" she asked.

"You're going back to London, Jane. You can take Richard's diary with you. I trust you'll mail it back when you're finished?"

"What—" He couldn't just tell her to leave...not after everything they'd been through. She wouldn't let him push her away from Stormclyffe or from him.

"Go home, Jane. You have no place here. An American scholar and an English earl? We both knew this wouldn't last, even though what we had was enjoyable." The frown on his sensual mouth tugged at her heart. Was he pushing her away to keep her safe? The man would do something stupid and noble like that.

"No. I don't believe you, Bastian. You don't have to push me away." She reached for him, but he shoved back his chair and stood, his body too far away.

"I'm not the marrying sort. I warned you that first day. But you never listen, do you? All you think about is yourself and your damned research. Well, I've given you everything. You can write your bloody thesis and go on your merry way. Leave me to deal with my family and my castle." His tone frosted her heart, but when his words sank in, fire exploded within her.

"Your family? I'm part of that family you arrogant jerk! I'm a Braxton. I have just as much right to be here as you do."

He arched one brow, the move subtle yet cynical. "All you have is a distant connection to the son of an innkeeper. Stormclyffe was never yours, *will* never be yours." He paused. "This discussion is over. I'll bring you back tonight, but Randolph will be taking you to the village first thing in the morning. You need to leave, Jane."

All fury fled and despair smothered her as she sucked in air. "But w—why?"

For a brief moment, his richly colored eyes softened before they turned hard as stone again. "Because these are *my* family secrets. Whatever happens here is for my family to deal with, not you."

A treacherous tear streaked down her cheek, and she brushed it away. He was killing her. Tim leaving her, calling her crazy, that betrayal hadn't been soul deep. Not like this.

"You know I have a connection to Stormclyffe. *To you.* I can help you. We can do this together."

He took a deep breath. Struck the fatal blow. "You've been a lovely dalliance, Jane, but I don't love you. Your purpose here is done, and there's no more reason for you to stay. Take your books and go home."

She could have sworn that the sharp clatter in her ears was from the sound of her own heart lying shattered on the floor in a million glittering pieces as he walked past her and left the library. She covered her mouth with the back of her hand to stifle the sound of a sob. Choking, she swallowed it down but couldn't stop the tears. She hated to cry, yet here she was, unable to control herself. Even after everything he'd done to her, she still loved him, and she hated herself for that.

. . .

Bastian lay on his back listening to the quiet night of the castle around him. A pang continually throbbed in his chest. He couldn't forget the look on Jane's face when he'd told her he didn't love her. She hadn't said a word to him all day after that. She'd retreated to her room to pack and had asked Randolph to send her dinner in her room. His butler had looked down his nose at Bastian as he'd explained that the young lady would be leaving at first light. But Randolph didn't understand. Jane had to leave.

If all of this madness was real, then Jane was in danger. He'd sent her away for her own good. It wasn't his fault that she'd believed all the lies he'd said to get her to leave. Because they were lies. He wanted her to stay here with him and never leave, but that wasn't possible. It was up to him to fix this, and he couldn't be worrying about Jane's safety.

With a frustrated groan, he rolled onto his side, trying to ignore thoughts of Jane and how he'd hurt her. He ought to be focusing on the problem of the witch and this curse. Who had moved Cordelia's body from the study?

With an irritated sigh, he slid out of bed. He needed to think.

There was one place he could go. He donned his pants he'd flung over the back of a chair in his haste to get free of them.

He reached the door, easing it open. His foot bumped into something on the floor. He bent down, hand searching in the dim light until it latched onto a book. When he straightened and examined it, an electric current shot through his hands again. This time it was almost painful.

Richard's diary. The book forced itself open and the pages flapped wildly before it snapped shut again in his hands.

Movement out of the corner of his eye caught his attention.

At the end of the hall, shadows lengthened, forming the shape of a man in breeches and a white shirt. A man with haunted eyes and a scarred soul who looked just like the man in the portrait in Jane's room and the one he'd seen in the ballroom after Jane had fled from him during their dance.

Richard.

The blood roared in his ears as he faced his dead ancestor. This was actually happening. He couldn't deny what his eyes were seeing.

The apparition raised a warning hand. *"She comes. She comes for your beloved. When the last bell tolls beyond the fall of midnight, your love will die."*

Bastian's throat went dry. His mouth worked frantically to find words, but none formed. Jane was going to die? The terror that filled him in that moment eclipsed anything he'd ever felt in his life.

"Beware the last bell."

The earl's ghost flickered, then winked out, leaving the hall empty.

"The last bell? Can't you tell me more than that?" he demanded of the vanished apparition. There were no working bells at Stormclyffe. They'd all broken years ago. Without their clappers, they could swing in the wind for all eternity and never make a sound. Richard's ghost was gone and didn't answer his question. Maybe he should go to the tower and make sure. Yes, he would do that. The last thing he wanted was for one of the bells to start ringing. If he could stop it, he would.

He headed for the drawing room, praying he wouldn't meet with another ghost. The truth kept smacking him in the face, and he'd been too reluctant to believe before he'd experienced that vision in the drawing and watched Richard die. But now he had to face it. Ghosts were real, and they were in his home, threatening *his Jane*. He would do anything to protect her. Anything.

He paused in the doorway of the drawing room and gazed at the painting of Isabelle. How like Jane she was, in face and form. But Jane wouldn't die; she wouldn't fall prey to the castle's predatory history that had torn his own family apart, driven his grandparents from their home for the last fifty years. She'd be away from this place in the morning.

"This is my home now. Do you hear me? Mine!" he snarled.

Let the ghosts come. He would be ready. For what could spirits do to a living, breathing human?

Nothing. He wouldn't let them. Leaving the main part of the house, he climbed the winding stairs in the tower at the far east of the castle where the three bells hung. The wooden door creaked open as he shoved his body against it. Wind whipped his shirt against his chest and he had to force himself to leave the shelter of the doorway to reach the bells. They were three tall, unmoving silhouettes against the moonlit night. As he approached them, he had to lean out over the structure that housed them. Beneath him was a forty-foot drop into an almost well-like pit. He ran his hand underneath each of the three bells, feeling for a clapper or anything that could strike the bell inside to make it ring. None of them had anything inside. They couldn't ring. That part of Richard's warning would never come to pass.

Sighing with relief, he turned away and headed for the half-open door to the tower that would lead him back down the circular stone stairway.

Dong!

The heavy ring of a bell tolled.

He spun on his heel and stared at the bells he'd just left. The bell closest to him swung slowly. Tendrils of pale light wove around its base as it rocked back and forth.

Dong!

Blood roared through him, drowning out all sounds except that one ominous *clang*, and the one that followed.

"Jane!" Without a second thought he ran, praying he wasn't too late.

. . .

Jane woke to the sound of weeping. A quiet, ragged gasping that had her hastily dressing and looking about for the source of the sound.

"Hello?" She nearly smacked herself in the forehead.

Great. Smart, Jane. Way to try and talk to the creepy thing crying in the dark.

It would have been easy to stay in bed, wait for Randolph to fetch her in the morning and take her away from this place and the man who'd just shattered her heart. But she didn't feel safe waiting around for whatever it was making that noise to come and get her. Sometimes being on the offensive was a safer move than being a victim—at least that was what she told herself.

She eased open the bedroom door and peeked out. The hallway was empty. Then she noticed the lights were moving, or rather *the shadows* were moving. Twisting, twining, coiling like phantom snakes, urging her to come toward them.

The muscles in her legs twitched, and she jerked forward, walking without control.

"No!" She struggled to regain control, but she couldn't, something was moving her forward. Not again...please not again. Just like when she'd walked to the top of the north tower. This time though, she knew with an icy certainty that she was going to die. Bastian wouldn't be able to save her, not this time.

Around her the world went mad. The tapestries she passed began to tear in long strips, as though a giant creature dragged its claws through the woven cloth. They fell in pieces to the ground. Invisible claws raked against the stones, leaving stark-white gouges in the rock.

If only she could scream, cry out for help. Bastian would have been able to hear. But there was no breath in her lungs, no ability to even gasp.

"He can't save you!" The screeching reply cut through her eardrums until she thought they might burst.

Darkness swallowed her whole, stealing all control, all consciousness.

Chapter Seventeen

Jane slowly regained consciousness. Her gaze took in the gray waves smashing against the stones below. Her chest was smeared with blood. But she wasn't hurt. It wasn't her blood. She whipped her head about frantically and realized in horror that she wasn't alone.

The figure of her nightmares, the creature that haunted and hunted her, stood a few feet away, holding a white dove in her hand, blood upon her palms. The putrid smell of death and decay invaded Jane's nostrils, making her eyes burn. Bits of flesh peeled away from the stark-white cheekbones of the monster's face. Its lidless eyes were ruby red and glowing. Jane bit her tongue, tasting blood as she sucked back a scream.

"You're Cordelia, aren't you? How are you even here? We removed your bones." Fighting to breathe each word, she sagged back against the massive rock she clung to on the cliff's edge.

"Clever girl, too clever. Bones were only part of what kept me here. The curse I cast upon Weymouth and his family is still unbroken. I will exist so long as it does." The terrifying creature laughed, and its horrible visage vanished, leaving only a lovely, golden-haired woman in a red cloak. It was as though the monster of her nightmares had never been.

"Why did you kill Isabelle and Richard? Why couldn't you just let them be?" They had been so happy, so in love, and this evil woman with her spells had destroyed them and every descendant afterward.

"Why did I kill them?" Cordelia only smiled, her eyes diamond sharp and just as cold. "I was the one he should have married. I was the *proper* choice. Not some ill-bred spawn of an innkeeper. She was no better than a servant compared to me. I couldn't let her live, not if I was to have Richard for my own." She walked around the rock, carving a line into the stone with a sharpened fingernail. "The fool was too stubborn to see I was better, that I deserved the title of Countess of Weymouth. I'd trained for it all my life, was supposed to marry him. My father had given him permission to court me, but he threw it away on some harlot who spread her legs for him."

As Cordelia talked, tiny red sparks danced around her, like angry hornets.

"So you succeeded, you killed them. Did you kill the maid, too?"

The ghost turned wicked eyes on her, devilry lighting them up. "Oh yes. Little Nessy, she was too friendly with the young heir to Stormclyffe. I saw the way he looked at her, hungry eyes, hands aching to touch her. A servant! I took care of her. Made her hang herself." Cordelia shut her eyes, a sinister smile curving her lips. "Such a lovely sound, when a neck breaks. *Pop!* Like snapping a twig. The only drawback is that death is instant. I would have loved for her to suffer."

Nausea rioted through Jane's stomach at the thought of the poor housemaid. Randolph had been right, and Nessy was one more victim.

"Now the last heir has come home."

"The last heir?" Jane was determined to keep that woman talking. Surely it could give her time to come up with a plan to escape. Or for Bastian to realize she was missing and find her.

"Yes." Cordelia's smile was full of rotted teeth. "All I need is to claim one male heir for my curse to be complete. The others escaped me. None of them would surrender to my will, not even when I stole everything they loved from them. I killed countless children, lovers, wives, pets. Anything that held value to a Stormclyffe heir, I stole it away. But none of the men would give themselves over to me. Bastian is the last one. And he will be mine."

"Did you kill his father?" Jane asked. Part of her had wondered and needed to know.

The witch smiled. "Oh yes. He thought he was so clever coming back here to mend the castle. But that's not what needed mending. I appeared before him on the road, intending to stop him. He swerved away from me and rolled that metal beast into a ditch. His life was gone before I could steal his soul away."

Tears stung Jane's eyes. Poor Bastian. It was a good thing he would never know the truth of his father's death. Better that he think it an accident than part of the true curse on this place.

"Why do you need Bastian? Why not leave him be?"

"I must have him, you fool. He is the last chance for what I want: to lay claim to Stormclyffe as mine. If I own him, I own this castle. He's more handsome than I'd hoped. Even more so than Richard." Cordelia's matter-of-fact announcement made Jane break out in a cold sweat. Cordelia was going to kill her. She was a threat to the ghost's claim on Bastian.

"What? No demand that he's yours? That you have the right to live? *How pathetic.* I'm going to kill you, just like Isabelle. But I'll push you far out, let you hit the water, break every bone in your body. You won't die right away, oh no, you'll drown while in intense agony. You will suck in the cold, salty water and perish. Then Bastian will be all mine."

"Like hell, you bitch! He won't agree to be yours." Where the rage came from, Jane didn't know. But for a brief second, the ghost's control over her weakened.

"Silence! He will agree to give himself to me if he thinks it will save your life." Cordelia snarled and cast the dove's body over the edge of the cliff, speaking in language Jane recognized as Latin. What little power Jane had recovered was torn from her again.

Her arms and legs belonged to Cordelia and her desires. The harsh pounding of the waves below was a siren's song to Jane, demanding she spread her arms wide and leap.

She clamped her fingers tighter around the boulder she leaned against. Her eyes closed instinctively, still resistant to the foreign power holding her in its grasp.

In the safe darkness of her closed eyelids, twin flames burst before her, growing larger. A vision of horror filling her mind, enveloping her. The flames morphed into bloodred eyes with slitted pupils.

"You will die…" The hiss slithered into her head and heart, its venom burning her from the inside out. *"You will pay for coming here. He is mine…forever mine!"*

Jane screamed as invisible talons slashed her chest and face. She let go of the rock to clutch her cheeks. The world pitched around her, and the pebbles beneath her shoes slid. The wind tore the shout of terror from her lips.

She dug her nails into the rocks and grass at the cliff's edge but couldn't catch a hold of anything. Her vision tunneled as the overcast skies winked out.

"Today you die!" The earsplitting laugh was as sharp as a thousand nails dragged over metal. It was a sound of pain or death. A sound of pure evil.

"No!" She gasped, her hands slipped free down a few

more inches on the edge.

This is what it feels like to die.

The racing heart, the blood roaring in her ears. No last moments of regret, no thought of loved ones or better days. There was only panic, terror, and then acceptance. Like climbing the stairs in the dark and reaching the top, expecting one more step. Only to have that moment of confusion and fear as you expected to fall before your foot struck the wood.

Bastian. His face filled her mind, the crooked grin he flashed her so often that made her knees buckle. The way he feathered kisses at her temples when he wanted an excuse to be close to her and knowing she adored it… She would never know such love again, and he would be alone. Her last sight would be the shrinking view of a cliff's edge far above her.

An explosion of light, followed by a shrill scream as piercing as a train whistle, cut through Jane as the lady in white appeared above her. Cold fury in her gaze, Isabelle looked at Cordelia and then leaped straight at Jane.

Jane sucked in a breath. Something soft, like mist, settled over her skin, sinking in with a tingling warmth.

"Let go, Jane. Let go," Isabelle's words were soothing, as though coaxing a babe back to sleep.

"She'll kill me, I can't!" Jane gasped, her voice breaking.

"Yes, you can. Trust me, Jane. Have faith. We must mend what once was broken. This is the only way. I've waited for you, centuries of waiting. Blood of my blood, flesh of my flesh, to have the strength to return and save us."

"Us?"

"Richard and me. Both trapped, kept apart. Broken."

"I'm sorry, Bastian, I'm so sorry."

The wind was the only witness to Jane's whispered apology as she let go.

• • •

Bastian reached the outcropping of rocks a few feet from Jane just in time to see her fall. The world slowed in that instant. The splatter of light rain plunked against the stones. A biting chill of wind burned his face, but all he saw was Jane.

Light bloomed at the cliff's edge. A silvery figure in a flowing white gown appeared, and without looking at him, dropped off the edge after Jane.

"We can save them. Trust in me." A deep voice jolted through him. He didn't have to look away to know that Richard's spectral form stood beside him.

"I trust you."

In that second, Bastian felt something merge with him. A ramming of power deep into his soul, his heart, as Richard took over. He could feel the other's presence in him, controlling every movement, every thought, but sharing it with him.

"Isabelle!" It was Bastian's voice but Richard's words.

Must save her. She must not die, not this time.

Bastian moved the last few feet to the edge where he'd seen Jane, guided by Richard's willpower as he dove onto his stomach, hand flailing out as he caught Jane's wrist.

• • •

Something hard latched around Jane's left wrist. The joint nearly snapped as she jerked to a halt. She gasped for breath and opened her eyes, hesitant to find her fate only delayed.

Above her, Bastian strained to hold her and not fall over himself. A pearly light shined in the black dots of his pupils. An otherworldly presence.

Inside her, Isabelle's spirit leaped for joy, and Jane's heart responded, pounding wildly against her ribs. They were two spirits united in her body. She'd let Isabelle into her, just as it seemed Bastian had let Richard into him. The ghosts were coming together because she and Bastian were holding onto each other. After two centuries of being apart, the lovers were touching through their descendants' hands.

So long, it's been so long my love. Isabelle's thoughts were heartbreaking and impossibly strong.

"Isabelle, reach for my other hand! Quick!" The veins in Bastian's neck stood out against his skin as he reached for her. Jane swung her free arm upward, and Bastian caught it, grunting in relief as he dragged her up and over the cliff. The second she cleared the edge, he fell backward, and she landed on top of him, their bodies locked in a fierce embrace.

Jane knew what she had to do, as if something inside her whispered how to fix everything.

"You're afraid, Bastian. You're afraid, and you're pushing me away, but I *know* you care for me."

The wind whipped around them, lashing at them along with the sound of Cordelia's shrieks. But a halo of brilliant light spread around them, keeping her at bay. She felt Isabelle leave her body, her presence instead enveloping Jane in a warm embrace.

He shook his head wildly. "You have to leave here. Tonight. Now!"

She took his face in her hands. "I love you, you arrogant jerk. You can't change that; you can't scare me off." Her voice was calm. Soft. But he heard her.

He turned away, squeezing his eyes shut as a grimace of pain crossed his features. "Jane, no."

She cupped his jaw, turned him toward her once more. She had to let go of her fear. To take a leap of faith and trust herself. "Bastian, I love you. And I know you're afraid. But don't be." She traced her fingers across his forehead. Along his jaw. "Please, believe me. I. Love. You." She emphasized those three words, refusing to let the howling winds drown them out.

She felt the tension rock his frame as myriad emotions warred on his beautiful face. "I can't. You have to go." The fear, so stark in his eyes, stilled her heart. They were both so alike, so afraid to get hurt, but they had to be brave. It was the only way.

"Say it, say what you feel. The truth. That's all we need between us. That's all we ever needed."

A hint of surrender shimmered in his eyes, and the tension in his body vanished.

"Do you always have to be so damned stubborn?" he growled and then leaned his forehead against hers. "I love you." The press of his lips was soft but filled with fire.

The halo around them coalesced into two points of brilliant light, which grew brighter and brighter, until they shot forward, directly into the heart of the beast that was Cordelia.

"No!" Cordelia screeched.

Above him, the witch's ghastly form burst into an inferno, a scream of rage tearing from her gaping mouth. A second later she disintegrated in a black sulfurous explosion, quickly blown away by wind from the sea.

"What happened?" Bastian gasped.

Jane panted and struggled to speak. "The curse…it wasn't about the castle. What once was broken must be mended. It was Isabelle and Richard. They'd been kept apart all these years." She wiped away the sea spray that mixed with tears on her cheeks. "We're their descendants. Our love brought them back together."

"Bloody hell, woman. Why didn't we figure out it was just that easy?" he muttered somewhat sarcastically, his head dropping back to the ground. One of his arms settled on her back, his hand patting her once, before he left his palm to rest there.

Too exhausted to laugh, she put her cheek to his chest, her whole body limp with relief. She wasn't sure how long they lay like that, but she couldn't readily break the feeling of security in his arms. Isabelle's spirit still pulsed inside her, and the ghost took control again, forcing her to sit up.

"Richard?" The name was rough on her lips, unexpected and raw.

He sat up, the blue light in his eyes still bright as he reached for her, enfolding her in his arms.

In that moment, four souls merged, connected and bathed in the light of each other. Jane couldn't breathe, the feeling was exquisite, pure pleasure, joy, surging through her, with her, around her.

"I've been so lost," Isabelle murmured. "I couldn't come home to you."

"Cordelia stole my dreams when she took you away." Bastian's arms banded tighter around Jane as Richard spoke through Bastian's voice. "We're lost no longer. My love…my heart."

Bastian dipped his head, his lips breathing life into Jane as the ghosts within them demanded one last kiss, one last second of mortality together. The love between Isabelle and Richard, that pure, undying devotion, was not foreign to Jane. Something like it had been growing inside her ever since she'd come face-to-face with Bastian. She loved him, loved him with a power and strength she had been so terrified to believe in at first.

She wanted to weep from the loss when Isabelle slid free of her body. All of that love, that strength was gone in an instant, but just as quickly her own love for Bastian replaced it. She raised her head and met Bastian's gaze. His eyes, no longer Richard's, seared her with heat and something softer. She smiled through watery eyes.

"I thought I'd lost you, Jane. When you went over…God, I don't know what I'd have done if I hadn't caught you." His words were so rough he seemed barely able to get them out.

There simply weren't words to express how she felt. The joy at being alive, the love for him burning hot as molten lava inside her.

It was madness. They were practically strangers. But she belonged to him, belonged *with* him.

"Are you all right?" His melodic voice with that sexy accent made her blood heat.

She nodded weakly. She cupped his face, relishing the way his stubble lightly scratched her palms. He was alive; she was alive. They were okay. "I'm fine. You?"

"I will be as soon as I can get you back into bed and inspect every inch of you myself."

Damn. The man was sex on a stick. Especially when he flashed that boyish grin and his eyes turned all melty and bedroomy. She sighed. She had it bad.

He chuckled, the sound soft and decadent, a veritable orgasm for her ears. It soothed her frayed nerves and pounding heart.

"Do you think it's over? No more ghosts?"

She kissed his cheek and hugged him, breathing in the scent of his skin mixed with the sea air. "Yeah, I do. The air feels different."

All around them the breeze moved, the blades of grass rippled and the waves rolled in against the cliffs. The heavy pressure of doom didn't layer the earth or burden the stones of the castle. Everything felt right.

"Let's get you back to the Hall." He helped her to rise.

She paused, looking back over the sea. Isabelle and Richard were back together, wherever they were, and Jane knew they were happy. How could they not be? All they'd ever wanted was to be together, in this life and the next. And they finally had that.

If only she knew what to expect of her own life. After everything they'd been through, did he love her enough to ask her stay with him? There was no more curse to keep them apart. Did she trust him with her heart? She wanted to with every fiber of her being.

He cupped her chin and turned her face to his. He ran the pad of his thumb over her bottom lip, the most tender expression softening his eyes.

"What are you thinking about?" He bent his head, feathering kisses along her jaw.

Her knees buckled, and she gripped his arms. She should say something hopelessly romantic. But she wouldn't make it too easy for him to seduce her. The man needed to learn to work for it. She grinned.

"I'm wondering how on earth I'm supposed to write my dissertation. There's no way I can explain anything that we've we learned or experienced. I guess I'll go with my backup topic on Richard III."

She relished the sound of his responding laugh.

"I can promise to take your mind off dissertation topics, at least for the next several hours." He captured her mouth with a heady kiss, his tongue tangled with hers as he deepened it.

When he released her mouth and threaded his fingers through her hair, she grinned impishly at him. "Only hours? How about days?" She waited anxiously to see how he'd respond.

"Days? If we're talking commitment, I'd like years." He stole another searing kiss. "Or maybe a lifetime."

Her heart thumbed at the base of her throat. "Is that your way of proposing?"

His lips curved in a slow seductive smile. "Perhaps I should write you a letter?"

"As long as I don't have to wait several months to figure out whether you actually meant it."

Her words had him dragging her into his arms, kissing her with all the fire and love she'd never thought she'd be lucky to have.

When they turned back toward Stormclyffe, Bastian slid his hand down her arm to take her own hand, lacing their fingers. As they approached Stormclyffe, she spoke.

"I suppose your gardener was wrong. He said that you coming here upset the balance between good and evil, but you fixed it."

He stilled, one foot raised above the first step leading up to the main castle door.

"Gardener?"

"Yeah," she gazed at him, worried by the confusion on his face, "a handsome man in his early thirties. He was really superstitious. He warned me away from the cliffs when I first saw Isabelle."

"Jane, I never hired one. I only had a temporary groundskeeper who helped with the deer, and he was a very old man."

"Then who…?" Jane glanced over at the rose covered archway. A shiver slunk up her back, raising the hairs on her neck as she focused on her memory of the man's features. He'd looked exactly like the man in the photo in Bastian's study. His father. Why hadn't she recognized him at once? She didn't know the answer.

Some things were best left alone.

Epilogue

"How do you feel…Dr. Seyton?" Bastian buried his face in Jane's hair, kissing her.

She laughed and turned in his arms, planting a nibbling kiss on his lips. "I like it when you call me doctor."

"Good, because I plan to call you that often. Earning your PhD is a big accomplishment. I've never been more proud of you." He raised her left hand to his lips. The small, elegant sapphire surrounded by a ring of diamonds glittered on her ring finger.

"And I have never been more proud to be with you, *my lord*." She winked at him, but the teasing was only a mask for the intense surge of love she had for him and knowing she would be soon be married to him.

"Can you believe in a month it will be official?" she asked.

He cupped her cheek, gazing down at her. "The day I call you mine cannot come soon enough."

"I'm already yours in every way that matters," she assured him.

The smile that curved his lips up made her heart skip a

beat. "Come. I want to show you something."

She followed him into the garden. Late spring had filled the castle grounds with an explosion of color and scents. Flowers bloomed, and birds chattered enthusiastically. Life was everywhere. She let her fingertips trail over the velvet petals of roses as they approached the old dovecote. He brought her to a stop and held her close from behind as he pointed to the top of the structure's roof.

A pair of doves peeked out from one of the holes. Their little heads bobbed as they studied the humans below. Then they emerged from the hole and perched on the thatch roof. Their white bodies snuggled close, and the small female buried her face in her mate's neck. He nipped her gently.

"How long have they been here?" she asked. Doves had returned to Stormclyffe Hall. Something inside her was both happy and yet sad at the same time.

"A few days. They appeared, just after we returned from your graduation ceremony."

"Really?" She stared at the birds, her heart beating a little faster.

The way the birds returned her gaze gave her an oddly familiar feeling. Her throat tightened.

"I'm so glad Isabelle chose to bring me here...to you." She covered his hands with hers where they rested on her shoulders.

"Then I owe her everything." He placed a lingering kiss on her temple.

Love grew inside her like an oil lamp coming to life, burning steadily, shining through a storm of emotions.

"I wish they hadn't died, Bastian. They were so in love, had so much life yet to live and they lost each other." It was the one thing that still haunted her. Isabelle and Richard had been robbed of the joy they deserved. It wasn't fair. She would have given almost anything for them to have the happing ending they deserved.

"I know, darling, I know," he murmured. "I think," he pointed to the doves, "that perhaps they have found a way to be happy." He turned her to face him. All around them the sound of the sea and the birds calling out encompassed them. He watched her, his eyes rich with promises.

"A love like theirs outlasts everything. A love like that…" His voice grew hoarse. "A love like *ours*…cannot die."

He bent his head, and she raised up on her toes to meet him in a kiss. Everything else faded away except that kiss, the love she felt, and the sweet coo of a pair of doves.

Acknowledgments

As always, there are so many people I would like to thank. First, the lovely, inspiring and supportive ladies of my Regency Romance critique group who are amazingly sweet to read and critique my books even when they aren't fully Regency. I'd also like to thank Berenda, Melissa, and Karen, who energize me with their love of reading and always ask when my next book is coming out. It makes me smile every time. I'd also like to thank my amazing editor Tracy, who loves haunted castles as much as I do and helped make this book the truly gripping, spooky, sensual story it should be.

About the Author

Lauren Smith is an attorney by day, author by night, who pens adventurous and edgy romance stories by the light of her smartphone flashlight app. She's a native Oklahoman who lives with her three pets: a feisty chinchilla, sophisticated cat, and dapper little schnauzer. She's won multiple awards in several romance subgenres including being an Amazon.com Breakthrough Novel Award quarterfinalist and a semifinalist for the Mary Wollstonecraft Shelley Award.

Lauren is represented by the wonderful Pam van Hylckama Vlieg from Foreward Literary Agency.

Check her out at laurensmithbooks.com, on Facebook at facebook.com/LaurenDianaSmith, on her blog, theleagueofrogues.blogspot.com, or follow her on Twitter at @LSmithAuthor.

Discover more Entangled Select Otherworld titles...

UNTHINKABLE
an *Evolution Paradox* novel by Nina Croft

Jake Callahan, leader of the Tribe, has always believed he's one of the good guys. Now, hunted by the government he used to work for, he's taking a crash course in being bad. He's forced to kidnap scientist Christa Winters. Someone is out to obliterate the Tribe and everyone associated with it, including Christa. Only by working together to uncover the secrets behind the past, can they ever hope to have a future.

QUANTUM
a novel by Jess Anastasi

Someone wants Captain Admiral Zander Graydon dead. Like yesterday. Zander's convinced his attractive assistant knows more than she's willing to say, and if he can stop running long enough, he'll find out exactly what she's hiding. Lieutenant Marshal Mae Petros is determined to keep her CO safe. Before she tips her hand, however, Mae has to figure out if the alluring man she's protecting is the real Captain Admiral Graydon. Or an alien shape shifting imposter.

SON OF THUNDER
a novel by Libby Bishop

Rune is the grandson of Thor, and just as strong. Exiled to the realm of Earth for nearly killing his brother–it was a little misunderstanding– he has to find a way to redeem himself so he can get back to Asgard. And when he lands—literally—in the bed of a fiery redhead with an FBI badge, he realizes that she may be the key to going home. But helping Liv hunt a killer has one big consequence—chemistry. He can't keep his hands off her, and there's no way they can ever be together.